MAKING MIDLIFE MAGIC

Forty is Fabulous 1

HELOISE HULL

Henwin Press LTD

Copyright © 2020 by Heloise Hull

All rights reserved.

No part of this book may be reproduced in any form or by any electronic or mechanical means, including information storage and retrieval systems, without written permission from the author, except for the use of brief quotations in a book review.

Any appearance to real people is purely a coincidence and should not be inferred.

If you are not reading this on Amazon, it has been pirated. This keeps your favorite authors from being able to write full-time if they aren't paid for their work. Please help keep your authors afloat. Thank you!

Making Midlife Magic

After finding my soon-to-be ex-husband together with my soon-to-be ex-assistant, I realize his "for better or for worse" didn't include my forties.

An extended vacation on a remote Italian island sounds like the perfect antidote to a midlife crisis—until I arrive. I'm expecting Chianti and pasta. What I get is a run-down bed and breakfast with the oldest Nonna in existence.

There's something about this island. Something odd. Like how everyone keeps calling me Mamma or how I'm the first tourist in decades.

And that's before I wake up to a talking chipmunk holding a glass of wine. He says I have something ancient in me, and for once, it's not my creaking joints.

When I finally discover the island's deepest secrets, I know my forties are about to be fabulous, if only I can survive long enough to enjoy them.

Fans of K.F. Breene, Robyn Peterman, and Shannon Mayer will love this new twist on paranormal women's fiction. For those who want experienced, seasoned characters in a whole new, magical world, book a trip to Aradia now! A little bit campy, a little bit epic, but 100% fun.

"Autumn is a second spring when every leaf is a flower."
-Albert Camus

Chapter One

I'D GIVE anything to be wrong in this moment—my full spectrum night goggles, my thermal camera, even my EVP meter. They never helped me find a real ghost anyway. I'd even allow my sniveling, ex-husband, who never loved any of my hobbies, to crow for the rest of his miserable life that he was right and I was wrong. Then, I wouldn't be staring at a dead body while its haunting residue floated inside my once very delicious glass of Italian red wine.

If only.

THREE DAYS Earlier

"WHERE'S MARLA? I need my wrong coffee order for the five hundredth day in a row," I joked. Nobody in the office laughed. Tough crowd.

That was fine. Nothing could derail me today. For the first time in almost a year, I'd booked an entire afternoon alone. A little treat to myself for dropping my twin sons off at college last week and only crying once, alone in their mixed-gender dorm bathroom.

Today, I'd finally use my gym membership to swim a few laps, maybe sit in the sauna, get a massage, and cap it off with one of those expensive wheatgrass açai protein shakes. Or whatever was cool these days. Just thinking healthy thoughts made it feel like those stubborn ten pounds were already melting away. Maybe tonight, I'd even feel relaxed enough to seduce Jim. With the lights out, obviously. It wasn't that I was overweight, merely a little *fluffy*, as my sons used to say when they were younger.

Oh no. Don't think about the boys. They're excited to be on their own. They had each other. It was fine. Everything was fine.

Before any seducing could happen, I needed to do a little grooming. I could thank my Mediterranean heritage for all the hair, I guess. Or curse it. I tanned easily, but good Lord, the hair. My eyebrows had only gotten more out of control with age. Whereas other moms complained about thinning eyebrows and cursed their zealous, over-plucking days, I'd given up on taming the beast a decade ago. Maybe two. If I was into honesty.

"Seriously, anyone know where Marla is?" I asked. Nobody looked up from their desk.

I may have been a senior sales associate at our insurance company, but everyone thought of me as Jim's wife. At some point, I'd stopped trying to impress them with sales numbers and nursed the hurt with Cheetos.

I checked my watch and considered my options. If I wanted to make my massage, I'd have to leave Marla a detailed email, text, and voicemail and then re-do everything tomorrow morning.

"Okay, if she decides to do her job today, have her call me."

Crickets.

I resisted the urge to strip and shimmy across a row of desks to see if anyone was alive, but I already knew the answer. This office sucked the life out of everything. Even the ferns and succulents we'd brought in to spruce up the place only lasted a month before they realized they preferred death to hanging out here day after day. I shuddered to think what a goldfish would do to escape.

I grabbed my purse and headed for the stairs. Step one: take more steps. I was already doing so well in this new phase of my life. October in St. Louis was among the best in the country. Upper seventies, blue skies, crisp air, and beautiful ridges of trees all going out in a fiery blaze of glory. I sucked in a breath. Beautiful.

As I reached for my car door, a gentle bump rolled across the asphalt parking lot. Odd. It was so slight, it could've been my imagination. Except a second, stronger wave rippled across the ground, and I hugged the car for support. My chest felt tight and panicky as fear squeezed my lungs. This was it. The big one.

St. Louis sat on the New Madrid fault line, and local authorities had been warning residents for years that it wasn't a matter of if, but when. What had they told us during earthquake drills in school? Something about doorways and… getting high? Or low? Open space, definitely open space.

The ground groaned awake like a beast rising from its slumber. I looked longingly at my car. Surely the parking lot wouldn't swallow it. Another surge threw me backwards, and I skidded across the ground, ripping my favorite skirt. Trees creaked and swayed, while animals chittered and squawked, all racing to take cover.

"Open space," I muttered, steadying myself between jolts. I rocked back and forth, trying to stay limber and sway with the rolling until it stopped. Consciously, I knew it had been a minute at most, but I felt trapped in a recurring loop of shaking and groaning.

Finally, it subsided, and I wondered how long I needed to wait for aftershocks. Also, why wasn't everyone streaming out of the building screaming?

I pulled out my phone for updates, giddy in my survival of the Big One. Scrolling only took a moment because there was... nothing. No mention. I paused to digest this. Maybe Twitter was slow to report because the earthquake took out important systems. Or something like that.

Whatever it was, I needed to check on my employees. My hair was disheveled and half of my leg had an angry looking scrape. A button had popped off my blouse, exposing my no-nonsense cotton bra, but after that quake, I doubted anyone else would look runway ready.

I pushed my way through the doors and took the stairs two at a time, adrenaline still coursing in my veins. When I burst into the office, my eyes bulging and my chest heaving, everyone's heads snapped up. Mouths dropped. Huh. So that's what it took to finally get their attention.

Rick, the office manager, guided me to a chair. "God, Ava, what happened?"

I stared at him. "Are you serious? An earthquake happened." Wildly, I searched for obvious signs of damage. No overturned filing cabinets, no broken glass littering the floor. Once again, nothing.

Rick's hand moved slowly to the phone beside us. "Maybe I should call Jim."

"He's not answering," I said. I ran to the window, dragging Rick with me. "There, see?" I pointed to a crack in the parking lot. From here, it looked like a giant scar.

"That is strange," he admitted, "but I think we would've felt it had there been an earthquake."

All eyes were on me in undisguised interest. Damn our open floor plan. Jim had insisted on it to keep an eye on everyone. I didn't realize the downside until now.

I patted my frizzy hair, feeling even crazier than it. "I think I need to go."

Rick looked concerned and almost reached out to stop me. I cut him off before he could usher me back to my office while he called 911.

"I'll see you tomorrow," I said and ran.

I hopped over the cracked asphalt—yes, it was cracked, I double-checked—jumped in the car, and turned the key. I drummed my fingers on the wheel as I screeched out of the lot toward home. This was all too weird. Thankfully the boys decided to go to school out of state, but I sent them a quick text message letting them know I was fine if something did hit the news.

Nothing seemed damaged as I drove. In fact, our neighborhood looked oddly normal. Two-story homes with three car garages were lined in a perfect row while black walnut and oak trees stood upright. I got to our house at the end of the cul-de-sac and froze.

Marla's red Subaru sat in the driveway.

My panic from the earthquake took a backseat as I double-checked the license plate, then my address. Not that I didn't know my own way home, but nothing about this day felt right.

I tried to remember if Jim had mentioned needing to borrow Marla. Had I forgotten? It was possible, but deep down, suspicions webbed my mind, spreading out and gathering all the evidence I had chosen to ignore for two years.

Like when the boys told me that Jim had talked to

Marla way too long at the last family day BBQ, or how she had a small smirk the last few times she'd gotten my coffee order wrong. I always thought it was because she was blonde and embraced the stereotype, but maybe I was mistaken. Maybe she knew exactly what she was doing.

Quietly, I parked, eased the front door open, and slipped inside.

I stood in the silence of the living room and took in the remnants of my life. While it no longer contained the twins, with their sticky finger prints and Curious George cartoons in the background, there was still an uneven workload. Work, laundry, dinner, sleep. Repeat.

That was my life.

I had already received my starter pack of menopause. Infrequent hot flashes. Weight gain. Chin hairs. Apparently, there was a thing called perimenopause, so that was frightening. I didn't feel old enough to be there. And yet, some days, I felt ancient.

A thud from the bedroom caught my attention, and a feeling of cold certainty washed over me. I knew what I was going to find, but I still wanted the reality of it. Seeing them together would make it easier in court. And easier to get over.

I made my way up the stairs, barely hesitating at my bedroom door. It was my bedroom, after all. Plus, it was like ripping off a Band-Aid. The quicker the better. I hadn't been in love with Jim when I married him, unless intense gratitude could be considered a kind of love. On the other hand, I never expected this.

The moment I saw them together in my bed, intertwined like two crabs wrestling in the surf, I knew I had made a mistake. This did suck. It was not like a Band-Aid in the least. This pain lingered. So I did the first thing I could think of. I threw a shoe at his hairy backside.

The shoe banged into the headboard, startling the lovers. Jim saw the shoe and, honest to God, cackled. No apologies, no groveling from my soon-to-be-ex-husband. Simply a, "Maybe if you went to the gym more, your aim wouldn't be so terrible."

Okay, so we were doing this.

"Maybe if you made more money, I'd have more time to go to the gym instead of having to work," I replied calmly. Then I threw a lamp. "It's every little girl's dream to grow up and sell insurance."

He caught it before it crashed to pieces against the wall. "Yes, your horrible life is all my fault."

"Well it's certainly not all mine!" Honestly, it was impressive how quickly we could morph into our old arguments, as if one of us wasn't butt naked with an audience.

A young voice piped up from the corner of our bedroom. "Maybe I should go."

I whirled on my soon-to-be ex-assistant, who was currently cowering and attempting to cover herself with my expensive bamboo sheets. I tried not to look too closely, but her taut skin with its astonishing lack of cellulite called to me like an annoying siren song. I couldn't stop gawking.

"What gave you that impression?" I asked. "Was it when I walked in on you blowing my husband or once the pottery started flying?"

Marla bunched the sheets in her hand and started feeling around for her underwear. "All of the above?"

I shot a fake finger gun at her. "I always said you'd go far. I just didn't imagine it to be so far up my husband's—"

"Ava." Jim gave me a reproachful look.

I couldn't believe it had come to this. Where was my happily ever after? My fairytale ending? When I married Jim, it wasn't stars in our eyes and moonlight in our wake. It was safety and security. But it was solid.

I should have known better. I guess part of me did. After growing up bouncing between foster homes and the street as a teenager, I always knew when the water got high, the survivors got higher. Now was the time to bail out.

As much as I wanted to fling more things at him, I was done making a scene. They didn't deserve the show.

"Fine. You know what? Stay. I'm going to remove myself from the conversation."

"And go where?"

"Anywhere."

Jim barked a laugh. "To do what? Ghost hunt full-time? I really don't know how I put up with your idiosyncrasies for so many years."

"Twenty," Marla interjected.

We both stared at her. She shrugged. "What? I have you down to buy flowers for your twentieth anniversary next month."

I threw up my hands. Oh, that was it. I went to the closet and yanked down the biggest suitcase we owned, and with no regard for what I was packing, threw in clothes and toiletries alike. "Marla, cancel the anniversary flowers and book me a ticket to Italy. I literally do not care where. I'm taking a vacation."

Thankfully, I had squirreled away a little money in a secret bank account from every paycheck over the past few years. As a wise psychopath once said, *"I will never go hungry again!"* Thank you, Scarlet O'Hara. Neither will I.

Marla, finally comfortable with something she knew how to do, dropped my sheets and grabbed her phone. I only peeked twice at her non-saggy, un-stretched boobs while her fingers flew across the touchscreen. Kids these days didn't appreciate what they had when they had it. She was in her mid-twenties, but anything under thirty felt like a kid to me.

Jim leaned against the doorway of the closet, arms across his chest. "So that's it?"

"That's it," I agreed.

"You're going to run away?"

"Sad that half of your money is running off with me to a beautiful, sun-drenched Italian island? Marla, make it an island."

"Yes, ma'am."

Jim rolled his eyes. "Take your money. I don't care if you spend it all on phony gauges, thermal cameras, and EMP recorders."

"It's EVP, you idiot."

"Whatever," Jim said. "Ghosts. Aren't. Real."

"Why do you hate my hobbies so much?" I held up a hand. "Wait, don't answer that. I don't care. Your hate is not my problem anymore. And you know what? I hate insurance. I'm never selling it again. Buy me out so I can go fan dollar bills over a dark, handsome stranger."

"Now you're just being stupid. What Italian man would want an over-the-hill forty-year-old woman like you? They have Italian women. You're nothing but a harpy, always harping on everyone around you about something. Why do you think the boys wanted us to leave so soon when we dropped them off?"

I clenched my hands to stop from breaking his nose. I did not have it in me to go with grace. "Jim?"

"What?" he asked. "Finally seeing the real light?"

"Go to hell, you over-compensating dick."

"After you—"

"Done!" Marla chimed in, looking to me for praise. It was all I could do not to throw the other lamp.

Chapter Two

I LOOKED up from my printed folder of reservations and check-in times at the dilapidated cottage on a rocky coast in the middle of a dirt road and swore eternal revenge on Marla.

It had taken a hefty bribe to get the boatman to come this far, and even then, he'd kicked me out before we'd gotten to the shore, throwing my suitcase into the surf after me. Now, I stood dripping wet in a courtyard while a chicken pecked at my feet and two goats bleated balefully for a snack. A series of raised garden beds took up most of the yard, but they were long past weeding.

I didn't think I could hate Marla more than I did when she messed up my coffee order day after day for two years or when she forgot to book a sales meeting with one of our most important clients. Or when I found her tangled up in my husband's arms. I was so wrong. Story of my life these days. Wrong place, wrong time, wrong, wrong, wrong.

I'd even been wrong about how much of my savings was actually mine in the impending divorce. It turned out that Jim carried a lot more debt than he'd let on, and I was on the twenty-year hook. My secret bank account would serve as a nest egg for a few weeks, but that was it. There went my attempts to *Under the Tuscan Sun* my midlife crisis.

At most, I could spend a long weekend in Italy and then hurry back to the States to find a job. Probably selling insurance. Worse, I wouldn't be my own boss. I'd have to start at the bottom of a ridiculously high corporate ladder at some other schlub's company and never get out of a cubicle again. I'd die there, hunched and curled over my keyboard, my phone perpetually attached to my ear with half-formed words coming out of my mouth when they found me. Then I'd haunt the cubicle for the rest of my existence, repeating, "I promise to halve your current raaaaate." It would be eerie and sad.

Or maybe just sad.

Was being with Jim really the golden years? That was a depressing thought. I wish I could say Jim was ugly, but he was perfectly symmetrical with a dimpled smile and blue eyes. I had let him sweep in like a white knight to save me all those years ago, giving up my freedom for security.

I hadn't pretended when we got married that it was deep, soul-shattering love. Rather, it was a way out of my troubles. As an orphan, I had a lot of troubles. Usually money, but there were a few brushes with the law, too.

Jim had cracked my heart with his infidelity, but he never held the power to break it. My heart was too well sealed for that. If he hadn't screwed me with debt, I would've sent him a fruit basket for setting me free. If only the cost of freedom hadn't been so high.

I looked one more time at my printed check-in documents to confirm.

Yep. Right place, but oh so wrong. Marla could have picked any island. Capri, Sardinia, or even Sicily would have worked.

The sun was already setting and my ride long gone. Unless I wanted to shell out more of my dwindling cash to charter a private boat back to the mainland at this hour, I needed to put on my big girl panties and stay for the night. Then I'd consider my options.

The bed and breakfast wasn't the worst thing. I could tell it used to be beautiful with tan paver stones, matte green shutters, and white wrought iron balconies over each window. But the paint was peeling and the white iron flaked with rust.

So, it was a tad run-down. The scenery was spectacular. Rocky outcrops, cypress trees, and the sweet smell of honey and saltwater mingled together as waves crashed against the rocks. Near the horizon, the water looked like a piece of turquoise glass, buffed to perfection. Someone had erected a stone statue of Venus to point over the waves toward the mainland. The statue was cracked and crumbling at the base, but the whole place could be picturesque with a little DIY work.

I had an immediate affinity for the statue. She could be me. I was her. Cracked and crumbling but fixable. Now, I only needed to figure out who I was. Not Ava Longsworth, mediocre insurance seller and mother of hellion boys. The possibilities, while not endless, were out there. I just needed to find me. Then I could work on fixing me.

Maybe I could get a job at a bookstore. Or a pet boutique selling fancy dog bones. I'd always liked animals, unlike Jim who claimed he was allergic. Anything to get experience running a small business and regrow my nest egg. I knew how to pull the bootstraps tight. The reflexes had grown a little rusty over the years, much like this house, but it'd all come back with practice.

I didn't have a choice.

A sparkle of something flashed out over the water. I

went closer to the cliff's edge. A dolphin? That would be a nice welcome. Dolphins were so playful and fun. And a sign of good luck. The beach was about fifty feet below, and there were tangles of pink and purple bougainvillea flowering at will. Like the statue, everything about this small island felt a little *wild*.

The flashing scales caught my eye again. So not a dolphin. Maybe a fish, then. The sparkling water was mesmerizing and soothing. I let myself sit down on the edge with my feet dangling. The waves crashed and receded with such regularity, it was like an expensive meditation class and therapy session all in one sun-soaked minute. Oh, to be as free as a fish—

"Hello!" a high-pitched voice screeched behind me.

I shook myself out of my jet-lagged fog, as a little old Italian nonna stood at the top of the cliff. She quickly hobbled over to me as I realized I had climbed half-way down.

The little nonna looked suspiciously over my shoulder for a moment. "You okay, girlie? You're not in a trance, are you?"

"No. Why would you ask that?"

"No reason. Come, let's get you inside. It's Mrs. Longsworth, *sì*?"

Hearing those words shook off the last spidering threads of my fog. Never again did I want to go by that name. "God no. Call me Ava. Ava Falcetti. It was my parents' surname."

"Ah, *parli Italiano*?"

"I wish," I said wistfully. I loved the musical, gesticulating language of the Italians, but my parents died when I was a baby. "Alas, I never learned it."

"You're a spring chicken compared to me. Plenty of time left." She put a wizened hand on my arm. Despite being hunched to almost half of my height and wearing a flowering night gown that swallowed her tiny frame, the woman had an air of old glamor around her. Her bone-white hair was carefully coiffed into a French twist, and she dripped jewelry. Gold bangles hung from her wrists, and gemstone rings adorned every finger.

"Thanks," I checked my details again, "Signora De Giorgi."

I left it at that. The only way I would learn a new language was if an alien body swapped with mine. Perhaps compared to this creaking, wrinkled, little grandmother figure I was young—but I had also pulled a muscle with that involuntary shudder back there, so she was literally the only person who would consider putting me and young in the same sentence.

"Call me Nonna. Everyone does. In an ironic sense. Never had children, let alone grandchildren." She took the porch stairs surprisingly fast and threw open the front door. "Here we are! I'm so glad you decided to stay at Villa Venus. There's only one other guest, and I haven't seen him in weeks, so the inn is practically yours. I live in the far bedroom, but the master suite looks out over the ocean. It's the best room in the villa by far. Aurick—that's the other occupant—doesn't like sunlight. He's from the northern countries, and I'm fairly certain that he's a vampire."

At the look on my face, Nonna laughed a wheezing smoker's laugh. "I'm only teasing, dear. He's eaten plenty of my garlic Bolognese. But I do believe he's allergic to sunlight. Now that I think about it, I should probably make sure he's still alive when we're done here."

I took in the villa as she spoke. Under the thick layer of dust, I could tell it used to be magnificent. The kitchen shelves were lined with brown earthen jugs and bowls, and thick cords of braided garlic and dried strings of pepperoncini hung from the cedar rafters. Bundles of rosemary had been placed over the lintels next to half a wheel of Parmigiano-Reggiano with a cheese knife stuck in the center. The windows were all thrown open to catch the sea breeze, and faded yellow curtains were drawn to let the sunlight filter inside. It wasn't five-star, but it was charming and picturesque. I had let Jim and his lavish ways lure me into five-star sensibilities. Turned out he had Lobster Thermidor taste on a popcorn shrimp budget.

But this? This was beautifully simplistic. This was perfection.

"Here's your room key and a house key," Nonna said, handing me two large, bronze keys. The weight of them in my hands felt like they could double as a deadly weapon if need be. "I don't ask that you keep curfews, just that you be respectful of how late you'll be getting in each night. We're early sleepers around here."

I laughed. "You don't have to worry about me, Nonna. I haven't been clubbing since I was eighteen. And I was a sad excuse for a rager then, too."

Nonna patted my cheek. Her hand was freezing and looked a little like a skeleton's appendage. "Don't underestimate the Adriatic sun, girlie. It brings back life."

A black and white portrait on the terracotta-tiled counter caught my attention. "Wow, is that your mother?" It was a beautiful woman with deeply glossed lips, thirties-styled ringlets, and porcelain skin. She held a cigarette in her mouth and stared seductively at the viewer. "She's beautiful."

Nonna laughed. "That's me at the height of my film career in Rome. I was a beauty, if I may say so."

"But that would make you over a hundred years old!" There must really be something to that Mediterranean diet mania. I mentally added *eat more olive oil and fresh fish* to my to-do list. And drink lots of red wine, of course.

"115 next month," she said proudly. "Once you spend time here, you'll never want to leave." She eyed me with a glint. "I promise."

Chapter Three

I SAT down on the bed and bounced on the handmade quilt. Luckily, I was alone on this rickety thing. If Nonna heard it squeaking, she might have a heart attack, and I refused to be the reason why a 115-year-old keeled over.

She'd set up flowers in a small vase on the dresser and left out lavender soap and a thread bare towel. Everything looked at least fifty years old, but it was adorable. Already I was falling in love. Maybe Nonna was right. Either the Adriatic sun was working its warm magic on me or she was with her Old World touches.

I plopped open my suitcase to see what I'd grabbed. "Good," I murmured as I pulled out my favorite yoga pants and racerback workout shirt, a few jeans, one sundress, a more formal dress, and three t-shirts. "Crap." No underwear except the pair on my ass.

It was only a weekend. I could survive. But I should probably let someone besides Jim and Marla know where I was staying. What if I suffered a weird, untimely death? Like me stumbling over the cliff after a bottle of Chianti. God, when had I become so fatalistic? It had to have been when the twins were born. Suddenly, everything could kill, and I started seeing danger around every unsecured bookcase corner and botulism-laced dirt the boys stuffed in their mouths as toddlers. The thought of the boys made me hope they were settled and happy in college. A sinister part of me wondered if Jim had gotten caught on purpose. The twins were gone, so what did it matter? We could finally pull the trigger on our fizzled marriage.

I flopped back on the bed. Like it mattered if he wanted to get caught or not. Here I was, a forty-something housewife and pretend-business woman in a run-down Italian villa on an island no one has heard of. And that was after surviving an earthquake that no one else had felt. No matter how many times I Googled it, I couldn't find any hint of it. Not even on a conspiracy blog. What if it happened again? I really should call someone. But who?

All of my close friends were *our* close friends. My girlfriends from my twenties had moved on, gotten married, had kids, and drifted apart. It happened all too often. Keeping in touch had become a once a year thing until it faded to nothing. I had no one.

That idea, that I truly was alone and starting over, hit me with the force of an ocean wave. It took me under and for the first time in years, I put my head in my hands and cried, a really good long sob that had been working its way out of my system since the morning I found Marla and Jim together. Maybe even before that.

The worst part? Jim was right about one thing. Hating my life wasn't completely his fault. I had done enough damage along the way, thinking if I worked harder or had more money, I could take a break. I could take that trip to Italy and indulge in pasta and wine. Now, here I was, but it felt wrong. Like I had only gotten here by getting lost. Jim's last words kept haunting me. *Over the hill. Forty-year-old woman. They have Italian women for that.*

I resisted the urge to pinch the extra inches around my hips that no spin classes could melt away after twins. Instead, I ran my fingers over the faint, silvery streaks on my thighs from my sudden growth spurt during puberty.

I'd done the late nights with sick babies, the no sleep for years, the potty training, the teenage rebellion years. Twin boys with a propensity for skateboarding injuries were no joke. I was supposed to be in the good part now. I could sit on the couch with a glass of wine and a bowl of popcorn and binge Ghost Hunters all weekend without feeling guilty. I'd suffered a horrendous childhood and appalling teen years, never getting the chance to attend college or even graduate high school, then chaining myself to a man I didn't love to provide some semblance of comfort and regularity in my life. Comfort I'd never had. Now, I was supposed to enjoy the peace and quiet.

"This sucks," I said quietly.

I stood up, feeling defiant and a little cleansed. So I said it louder. "This really freaking sucks!"

"What sucks?"

I yelped and spun, frantically searching for the voice, but I didn't see anyone.

"Hello?" I asked cautiously. "Nonna?" At the silence, I tried again, whispering, "Aurick?"

In every book I'd read, vampires had to be invited in before they could suck your blood. Did it count if Nonna had already invited him into the villa or was my room protected, too?

"Hello?" I asked one last time, but no one answered, leaving me waving a bar of lavender-scented soap into thin air, the hairs prickling on the back of my neck.

Chapter Four

AFTER ANOTHER GOOD CRY–THIS time about the fact that I was losing my mind in addition to everything else in my life—I took a short, lukewarm cat bath in the bathroom sink down the hall. It was the best the house could do, but it felt good to scrub the last thirty-six hours off of my skin. Then I wandered back into the kitchen, my stomach growling.

I heard two voices, Nonna's and another deep and rumbly. I expected to meet mysterious Aurick, but when I turned the corner, I found Nonna conversing with a chipmunk.

The tiny creature took a hazelnut from her hand and gestured at me. I squeaked and pointed, which apparently offended him. The chipmunk gave me an intense once-over and scurried off. If chipmunks could read souls, he would have imprinted mine in his memory.

Nonna brushed it off, like it wasn't the weirdest thing in the world to be conversing with a chipmunk. "Do you feel better?" she asked. "I've been waiting for you."

"You have? Was that...?"

She waved her hand through the air. "Yes, yes. A chipmunk. He keeps me company."

"Was he..."

"Eating from my hand? Yes, he's grown to trust me over the years."

I was going to say *talking*, but I didn't push it. I didn't need Nonna worrying about my sanity. "What's for dinner?" I asked.

"That depends on what you order."

"You run your inn like a restaurant?"

"No, of course not. You'll be eating at the local taverna in town."

"Nonna, I really don't think I'm ready to go meet people," I protested. Neither the WIFI nor my cell service worked out here, and anyway—I was going crazy. Strangers did not need to be subjected to that. "I'll find something little here on my own, and then I'm going to collapse."

"Nonsense. A young lady like you should be out with others your age."

"I'm forty. I have wrinkles that could be considered young."

Nonna took me by the elbow and led me to the door. "I'll go with you. This crisp air is just what my old bones need. Besides, it's aperitivo hour!"

She dragged me to a lime green Vespa. It was the kind I'd seen in television ads, usually with a young, beautiful woman with her hair flowing in the wind and a smile lighting up her face.

Nonna handed me a helmet, muttered something under her breath, a prayer perhaps, and creaked awkwardly on board. I climbed up after her. Having only met her an hour ago, I couldn't very well start mothering her. If she wanted to break her back, that was her business, but I really wished I could just drive her old bones into town.

"*Andiamo!*" she shouted into the salt wind, and after a few revs, we were off.

A week ago, I never would have believed I'd be hanging onto the oldest woman in the world's sagging waist on a tiny, Italian island while my husband shacked up with my assistant. It was too absurd. So instead of thinking, we rode. I wished I'd brought my Fitbit. The last time I'd worn it—a passive aggressive birthday gift from Jim—I'd accidentally connected it to Facebook and then everyone knew I'd only walked eighteen steps that day. Approximately.

"Why is this place so quiet?" I asked, shouting over the wind. There were barely any tourists and everything in town felt medieval. In fact, I was positive the only upgrades on this island in the last hundred years had been plumbing and electricity.

"We used to be a tourist destination, back in the 70s. That's when I started running Villa Venus. I quit acting during the Nazi and Fascist business and was considered too "old" to get back into it at forty. Pah. What do men know about age?"

I nodded. What indeed? Forty was absolutely the new thirty. I sometimes needed an aspirin to get up in the morning, but I could still touch my toes—with a bent knee. It wasn't like I was that bendy in my twenties, either, so I could hardly blame that on turning forty. Yoga hadn't helped in that department.

"So what happened?" I asked.

"About a decade ago, strange things transpired. Ghosts and apparitions appeared. Things went missing. Tourism dried up and people blamed *malocchio* curses."

"Seriously! Like what?"

"One night, all of the island's goats were found feet in the air, dead as a doornail. The scariest part?"

I bent closer to her shoulder to catch her words. Nonna's voice had this forceful quality to it that compelled you to pay attention. It was probably what made her such a good film star.

"Their eyes had turned a milky purple-white." Nonna laughed her scratchy smokers' laugh, breaking the spell. "All nonsense. Except for the goats and stomach aches. I think it was something in the water that made everyone sick. Sewage or rot of some sort. Anyway, we Italians adore a good ghost story, true or not."

"Me too. I actually ghost hunt as a hobby," I said. "It must be the Italian in me!"

Nonna had that glint in her eye again. "Oh, do you, girlie? What a coincidence."

I couldn't deny the shivers that went up and down my arms at her words. Or how nice it felt to feel spooked. I loved it. The spine-tingling chills and the impulse to look over my shoulder always made me feel alive. Probably because I'd been living half-alive before that.

I remembered the voice in my room. Maybe it was Nonna herself, trying to scare me before she told me this story. I'd only just met her, but I wouldn't put anything past this wily old woman.

Nonna turned a corner and putted into a town square. The village had kept its medieval city planning with all the buildings surrounding a central square with a fountain tinkling in the middle. Nonna kicked out her stand like a pro, clipped her helmet around the handlebars, and hobbled to an old stone structure with candles flickering in the window. A creaking wooden sign read, Taverna Est. 1260.

It had little round tables with two chairs set up to people watch, and dominoes and checkers on a few of them. Each table had a bottle of wine and a tea light. I rubbed my hands eagerly. Now this was what I came to Italy for. Jim might have been in bed by eight p.m. every night to watch the news, but I was going to enjoy myself.

I pointed to the wood-smoked sign. "This little island has had the same bar since the thirteenth century? Wow. And I thought you were old."

Nonna chuckled. "They used to sell 'We survived the Plague' t-shirts, but they're gathering cobwebs in the corner now. I should get you one."

She ushered me through the thick, wooden door with iron nails the size of my eyeballs. Guess that meant no fae could enter. I loved imagining those delicious thoughts. It was so much fun to sink into a fantasy world. Nonna knocked on one of the iron nails as she entered.

"What was that?" I asked.

"Italian superstition. Instead of knocking on wood, we knock on iron. *Tocca ferro.*"

I followed her lead and gave a little rap with my knuckles as I passed. Inside, it was dark and smoky and louder than I expected. It appeared the whole town came here after work to have drinks and an early dinner.

As if she read my mind, Nonna said, "Everyone likes to gather for apertivo hour on Thursdays and Fridays. Lucky you, girlie. It's Friday."

I had completely lost track of the days, which was precisely the way I wanted it for now. Let Monday come. I'd figure out life then. For now, I was going to enjoy my Italian weekend.

Nonna went straight to a table that seemed to be

reserved for her and held up two fingers. "*Due limoncello per favore*, Marco!"

"*Sì*, Signora Nonna!"

The whole taverna was alive with friendly banter. Now I understood why the island had appeared dead on my arrival. All of the life was beating in the center of the town. Candle wax and scuff marks laced the tables, while the smell of grilling lamb chops and acidic lemon scented the air. Even if it was a tourist trap with a fake date—thirteenth century, come on—it felt real.

People milled up to talk to Nonna and slyly pry. I got the feeling that while Nonna was an institution, many were a little wary of her, and they were definitely wary of me. As she held court for a few minutes, Marco bustled up with a tray of cloudy, yellow limoncello and little plates of grilled bread with something golden white smeared on them.

"Marco makes the best goat cheese butter," Nonna said. He had to have been nearing sixty with a grizzled face and a mane of reddish-gold hair mixed with salt, but she made him blush like a sixteen-year-old.

"*Grazie*, Signora Nonna. I have tomatoes marinated in olive oil and herbs, too."

I noticed there was only one person who hadn't come up to say hello and pay their respects. A tall, hulking figure of a man, hunched over the bar. He was alone.

Nonna followed my gaze. "Oh, that's Luca," she said craftily. "All the women love him."

"Easy to see why," I said before I had time to stop myself.

Nonna gave my cheek a soft pinch. "Yes. A fine, strapping man. He came a decade ago to get over the death of his first wife. He mostly keeps to himself outside of being the town's self-designated *polizia*. He sweeps in, arrests the drunks, tickets over-eager goats for tearing apart garden beds. That sort of thing. All with a frown. We all think he needs a good woman to loosen him up, but he won't hear of it. Too honor-bound to his dead wife."

"Why do I get the feeling you're trying to play matchmaker?"

Nonna gave me a smile. "Humor an old woman, *per favore*."

"I can't believe I'm saying this, but why not?" It was one weekend. If he was a total boar/bore, it'd be *ciao*, see you never come Monday morning. I walked up, my confidence nosediving with each step. My wing woman was a 115-year old bed and breakfast owner. Who talked to chipmunks. What was I thinking?

Up close, Luca was over six feet with dark brown hair graying at the temples. A few loose pieces dangled over his forehead. It was thick and luxurious, and for a second, I heard a loud droning in my ears as I imagined running my fingers through it—and up and down his gorgeously golden skin and around his square jaw. Hello, hunky Italian man.

It took a second to realize he'd been asking me something in rapid-fire Italian. "I'm sorry what?" I asked at his questioning face. He seemed shaken by my sudden presence.

"Ah, American." His thick accent coated each word, while his chocolate brown eyes narrowed in confusion. "What is an American doing on Aradia?"

"Vacation," I said innocently, attempting to ooze seduction. I couldn't quite remember. Was it rim the top of the wine glass with a finger or a thumb or do something with the bottom? I settled for biting my lip slightly in the corner.

Luca watched me intently, as if every movement I

made was something exquisite to be savored. The gaze invited me to stare back.

"So, I heard you were the town's law enforcement. I'm Ava Falcetti," I stuck out my hand, liking the taste of my old name on my tongue.

"Planning on committing a crime on your holiday?" he asked, amusement lilting in his voice.

"If I got to speak to you, maybe I'd consider it," I said, cringing the whole time. Lord, I was out of practice.

"I suggest you don't. Italian courts of law are notoriously sexist."

"Thanks. I'll keep that in mind the next time I get an urge to kidnap a goat."

Luca continued to stare with an expression that could have hid multitudes. Or just attitudes. I didn't know what to make of this man. He was delicious to look at, with rippling muscles and fathomless eyes, but there was something else underneath his casual chinos and button down shirt. Something a tad dangerous. Although, I had to admit that part was the most alluring of all.

Luca set down his half-drunk beer and some Euros. "*Grazie*, Marco," he said in a deep, vibrating accent that had my insides quivering. "Stay safe, Signora." He nodded his head at me and left.

I winced. Ouch. So, Jim was right. I was over the hill. I couldn't tell which part hurt more—the Jim being right part or the over the hill part. But why should it matter what one man thought of me? I may not be in tip top shape, but I wasn't completely out of it. I had my thick, long, dark hair with only a handful of grays—and my dignity. Or had I just lost that too?

Before my thoughts could spiral to the dark side, the wooden door banged open.

"*Il fantasma!*"

Everyone's heads snapped up like they'd been pulled by a string. A young boy was heaving on the doorstep, his eyes dilated and his cheeks red. He pointed with a shaking arm outside, barely able to speak.

"Ghost!"

Chapter Five

INSTANTLY, the taverna cleared of people. They all looked terrified. Those old ghost stories had clearly left an impact.

Nonna hobbled through the stampede and grabbed my elbow. "Come on, girlie. Time to go."

"Home? I didn't think you believed in all that nonsense."

"*Certo che no*," she admonished me with a finger wag. "Of course not. We're going to see this ghost!"

"Oh yes, I'm the silly one," I said, but I grabbed my purse and followed. Shoot, I wished I had my recorder and night vision goggles. Or a thermometer to measure cold spots. Anything but an iPhone camera.

"Do you think it's there?"

"Do you?" she asked, moving fast for a centenarian.

"I hope so," I said honestly. "What were the sightings before? Just orbs or actual apparitions?"

"Apparitions. Italy has too much history," she complained. "If it's not Roman, it's Renaissance. If it's not Renaissance, it's Napoleonic. Lately, they say a man in a black plague masque has been hovering around, but the last sighting was a while ago. That one was a bit creepier. He never spoke. Only stared."

We made our way to the center of the square. At first, I didn't notice anything out of the ordinary. Just the townspeople hovering near the light, talking low. The gurgle of the fountain was the loudest thing in the square. Then a cat yowled and shot across the courtyard. A chill spun up my spine and peppered my skin despite the warm fall air.

"Feel that, girlie?" Nonna whispered.

I nodded, too terrified to speak. Something was actually here!

All at once, a burst of cold shot through the courtyard, and something materialized to my left. My breath turned to ice; I could reach out and shatter it with a finger.

By the feathered cap and tights, it was a Renaissance ghost. He circled around me, back and forth, floating a few feet above the ground. The crowd gasped, but no one took out their phones. That was weird. If I could get my muscles to move, I could capture all of this.

"Who… who are you?" I chattered.

The ghost stopped in front of me. His skinny goatee and clipped mustache jiggled as he tilted his head back and forth. Like he was considering me. I hoped it wasn't the alcohol affecting me, giving me weird visions, since this was one of the greatest moments of my life.

"*No, no, no. Mi sono infatuata di te. Sei bellissima. Dio mio, ho un debole per te!*"

"Nonna," I hissed out of the corner of my mouth. "What is he saying?"

"Nothing important. He thinks he's in love with you, he's going weak for you, etc. Ask him again what he wants."

"What do you want?" I asked, my voice shaking only a little.

"You speak English. That's okay. We'll figure it out. But what else to uncover? What are you, my delicious cannoli? I would suffer another round of the Inquisition just to see you again." He sniffed around my hair. "And to plumb your depths."

I shivered. "Your voice…"

"Yes, *dolce pasticcino mia?*"

"Were you at Villa Venus?" I dropped to a whisper. "Spying on me?"

The ghost winked. Honestly. I said that sentence. A. Ghost. Winked. At me, no less.

"*Non posso vivere senza di te!*" he exclaimed, bowing and kissing my hand. His incorporeal body couldn't touch me, but we all got the gesture.

Nonna scoffed. "You're already dead, so I think you did live without her."

The Renaissance ghost glanced at Nonna and recoiled. His form flickered like a bad television reception, and he skyrocketed for a moment before floating back down. He let out a string of Italian sentences and curses that I had no hope of catching. Until the last word.

He lifted a bejeweled finger at Nonna and hissed, "*Strega!*" before vanishing in a gust of arctic air.

Chapter Six

THAT NIGHT, I dreamed of Italian pools of pasta and rivers of red wine. I floated in the Adriatic, letting my hair drift around me like some mermaid or nymph. The waves were soothing and the salt cleansed the wounds I'd acquired from forty years of life. The late carpooling days, the hot mess yoga hair, the attempts to be funny that fell flat at soccer practice. "How 'bout them balls" should really be left to the professionals.

Now, I didn't care if I made people laugh. I didn't have to worry about being late to pick up every Axel and Rose my boys befriended. (True names. This is what happens when Guns N' Roses fans become parents.) Before I'd left, I saw on Facebook that an old friend I'd known from elementary school was pregnant again with her second husband. At forty! I couldn't imagine. Couldn't fathom. No and thank you. I didn't consider myself over the hill. I had more grays than five years ago and got a secret little pleasure every time I brushed my hair and one fell out, but I wasn't infirm. I merely couldn't imagine giving my body over to another tiny human again.

Jim was a jerk because he wanted out. Because he'd gotten bored, and instead of trying to fix things, he took the easy way. An affair. And that rejection would make me stronger. If only I could stop from drowning.

Water flushed over my face and filled my mouth. Soon my lungs expanded and contracted as I flailed in the sea.

"Help!" I gurgled, while a beautiful woman braided her hair on a rock. She watched curiously.

My nose went under, and I floated like a still life through the warm waters. I could feel the end coming, warm and unforgiving. Then I did a rather impressive jolt, spasmed off the bed and clunked to the floor, where I laid tangled in the sheets, my head against the wooden planks.

"Just a dream," I told myself, but it felt so real. I coughed and sputtered. Had I been choking on my own spit?

"Here, take this." A chipmunk handed me a glass of deep red wine. "Blessed water. It will take the edge off."

I screamed again and hit my head against the metal bed frame.

"Shhhh. You'll wake the rest of the dead with that screaming," said something translucent, floating behind the chipmunk's twitchy ears.

I screamed again. I could swear this ghost looked like...

"Nonna, is that you?"

"Yes, girlie."

"Why are you hovering over me like—"

"Like a ghost?" she supplied.

I could feel my pulse beating through my neck, my heart rate skyrocketing into dangerous stratospheres. Twenty years of ghost hunting and the most I could claim was some odd noises and a few cold spots. Now this?

"Tiberius is my familiar," the ghost of Nonna said, as

if that explained anything. "I'm a witch. Your Renaissance romancer was right about the *strega* bit. That's Italian for witch."

I pinched my arm to make sure I wasn't dreaming. It left an angry, red welt, and it hurt. "Is this the part where a big, hairy giant comes in and tells me 'Yer a witch, Ava'? Are you my Hagrid?" I asked seriously.

"I don't know who that is, but Bigfoot isn't available. I guess I could put in a request for a troll or something."

"Lord, no. Just... no," I said, putting my hand to my head. Clammy, moist. I wished I was a doctor so I could diagnose myself. Nightmares, visions, scratch that—delusions—and an erratic pulse.

In the middle of my self-diagnosis, the chipmunk jumped up on my leg and began sniffing me. "Good, because I don't think you're a witch."

I screamed again. "It really does talk!"

"Of course, he talks," Nonna admonished me. "Take a drink of wine. It will help, I promise."

I took a long swig as Tiberius continued his investigation. He crawled up to my nose, and I got my first good look at him. On the surface, he appeared to be a normal chipmunk, but his eyes looked older and wiser than any rodent's I'd ever seen.

"What are you sensing?" Nonna prodded him.

"I'm not sure. Not a witch, but something. Surely she can't be a MILF." He put his paws together and rubbed them. "A mystery. I adore mysteries."

"Yeah, I used to think I did, too," I grumbled. "I no longer believe that."

"Well, you don't have a choice," Nonna sputtered, her image flickering as bits of her ectoplasm splashed into my wine. "Something's murdered me, and you need to figure out who!"

I tossed my wine against the plaster wall where it splattered. It hadn't taken the edge off anyway. "Murdered?" I repeated, hoping I'd heard her wrong.

"Yes, murdered. Now, grab a weapon and go find my body."

"Fine," I said, grabbing the vase of flowers and dumping the water and petunias on the ground. "But I really hope this is some kind of sick joke."

With a cautious look around the corner of my door, I inched along the wall, feeling my way to Nonna's room. She floated behind me, giving me orders like a war general. All in all, she seemed to be in her element. "You'll need to avenge me, girlie. Get a stake and some Holy Water from the basilica. Garlic doesn't work, but this has to be Aurick's doing."

"Will you be quiet?" I hissed back. "I'm trying to find your body.

"It's there alright, girlie. Blood splatters and everything. Prepare yourself. It's gruesome."

"Why do you look so happy about that?"

As we passed the kitchen, I grabbed a butcher's knife, just in case. What the hell I would do with a butcher's knife was another question.

With the tip of my blade, I nudged the door. It swung open with a loud creak, and I managed to only pee myself a little. Damn bladder control. Why couldn't I have gone to the bathroom first? Oh right, killer on the loose.

"Stop lollygagging and get in there." Nonna floated ahead—and let out a bloodcurdling shriek.

I swooped into the room, baring my weapons. And found nothing, except for an ancient woman that looked perfectly asleep. Tiberius hopped up on the bed and peered into Nonna's face.

"Where's the blood?" I asked.

"It's here somewhere," Nonna said, doing circles around her body.

I took a deep, calming breath and cautiously approached. "Are you sure you didn't pass peacefully in your sleep from old age?"

Nonna whipped around, ruffling the curtains and my nightdress in a chilling mist. Her eyes sparked black and she howled. "It was not peaceful!"

"Okay," I said slowly, trying to back out of the room. "Maybe you suffocated?"

"You seem to know a lot about how I died," Nonna said, blocking my way like an ephemeral quarterback. "Doesn't she, Tiberius?"

The chipmunk bobbed his head noncommittally.

"What?" Nonna demanded.

"On second thought, you do look pretty peaceful," Tiberius reasoned. "Maybe there's some other explanation for why you can't move on."

And just like that, the chipmunk became my new best friend.

"Because I was brutally murdered! Now hurry up, we have to cleanse the villa of evil."

"Not to be obvious or anything, but your *dead body* is still lying in your bed. Shouldn't calling Luca be the first thing we do?"

"No!" Nonna flickered again erratically. "You have to pretend like nothing is wrong until you find my murderer."

"You have got to be kidding. This is a joke, right? I'm the dead one. That must be it." For the tenth time since arriving, I felt my forehead for a fever. "Did Aurick kill me? Is there even an Aurick here? Did you kill me?"

"If I had a body," Nonna said, "I would have slapped you three sentences ago. If anyone did the killing, it was you."

"Ladies, if we could pause the murder accusations and think rationally," Tiberius tried.

Unfortunately for the chipmunk, we both ignored him. Nonna began describing an elaborate cleansing ritual that I needed to do immediately, but something had caught my eye. "Then, cut a lamb's hindquarters from north to south, and—What are you doing with my dead body?"

By now, I was used to Nonna's ghostly theatrics. Instead of taking notes like she wanted, I inched closer, the butcher knife dangling at my side. "If you're dead, why is your chest moving?" I asked.

Nonna paused and cocked her head. "Oh. Oh no."

I narrowed my eyes. "Oh no, what?"

Tiberius rolled his chipmunk eyes and bounded off for the kitchen, announcing he needed a snack.

"This is on me," Nonna said.

"What's on you?"

Without answering, Nonna glowed a brilliant, azure blue and sank into her body. Then, she sat up with a gasp, her hair still in hot pink rollers.

I put on my mom voice. The one right before Dark Night Batman level. "What did you do?"

For once, the indomitable woman looked meek. "Astral projection. I can move between planes, but the older I've gotten, the harder it is to control. Especially when I'm sleeping. Or approaching orgasm."

"Oh good God, that's—yep, I'm going to be sick." I put a fist over my mouth.

"What?" Nonna eyed me, her sass firmly back in place. "Older women can't have a sexual identity? Won't you be sad in seventy years."

I shuddered.

"First things first," Nonna announced, sliding out of bed in her flowery nightgown. "You need to cleanse the kitchen after this disaster. Go grab my salt and sprinkle it in the four corners." When I didn't move, Nonna clapped her very alive, very mottled hands. "Go on, girlie. Up you go. Salt is in the bowl by the hearth. Then broom it towards the center, pick it up, and toss it out back."

"I'm not cutting up a lamb leg."

Nonna waved her hands. "We'll discuss it later."

"Nonna, there is no later. This has all been weird and almost to the point where I'm considering committing myself, but I can't stay. I have to go home in two days." Now that the chipmunk and the astral projection—or whatever that was—were gone, I could almost believe I'd dreamt everything. That felt safer, anyway. "And book an extended session with my therapist," I muttered.

"You can't leave," Nonna exclaimed. "I need you to help me run Villa Venus while we figure this out."

"You weren't murdered. There's nothing to figure out."

"Strange things are afoot. They've been for decades now, but I haven't been able to find the thread connecting it all." She moved around me, taking me in from every angle. "But maybe you can. You heeded the island's call after all."

"I didn't heed anything. I indulged in a midlife crisis."

"Nonsense. The island called and you came. You should feel honored."

"Here's where you're going to tell me this wasn't a coincidence? That my slutty assistant did this on purpose?" Although, in the back of my mind I pictured the earthquake only I had felt, and I couldn't help but wonder. Was there something legitimately supernatural occurring?

Nonna put her hands on her hips and pierced me with a severe glare. "You talked to a chipmunk and you can't believe a simple conjuring spell is possible?"

I leaned out the door and saw Tiberius struggling to

refill another glass of wine in the kitchen. "I think she's going to need this first," he huffed.

And once again, the only sane one in the room was a chipmunk.

Make that a lifetime of extended therapy sessions.

NONNA DIRECTED me the entire time I performed the cleansing ritual. She claimed she was weak after projecting for so long and could barely lift her arms to fix her hair. Now she had me banging around on the ground, looking for a two-quart pot while she unrolled her curlers and used an ozone-depleting amount of hairspray. "Fill it three-quarters of the way with water. Okay, now add three cinnamon sticks, three whole cloves, one teaspoon of the swept salt, and half of a lemon. Level that salt! Magic needs to be precise, girlie."

"I'm not a girlie!" I exploded as she made me re-measure for the third time. "I'm a grown woman who sees ghosts and astral projections apparently."

"Level it," she repeated firmly. "*Buone*. Bring that to a boil, then reduce to a simmer for two hours. Then leave it to cool, fish out the lemon, and funnel it into a spray bottle. You'll mist the whole house."

"Is that all?"

"No, but I'll turn you into a proper *femmine di casa* yet."

"What's that?" I asked, afraid of the answer.

"A proper domestic Italian housewife."

Domestic implied there were also feral housewives. Now I had a life goal. "Sorry, but that ship has sailed. I will never go back to being a proper anything." Just thinking about all the time I'd spent cleaning toilets or sifting through dirty jockstraps made me shudder.

"I admire that, girlie. I really do. But you need to learn to be a proper witch, despite absolutely no training."

"What if I'm not a witch?"

"What if you are?" she countered.

"Would I be able to do all that?" I motioned with my hands like flying. I was starting to get genuinely interested. Or perhaps just chilled out by the second glass of wine.

Tiberius and Nonna exchanged another glance that spoke a thousand words. None in any language I understood, of course.

"Most witches do not astral project. It's a special talent of a special breed. Later, I'll have you dig up my grimoire and start teaching you the basics. Eventually, you can meet the girls, but I must say they've been slacking lately. No wonder this town is getting overrun with vengeful Renaissance faire ghosts. Oh, and I put a little spell on you to open your eyes when you arrived, but it won't last. If you want to stay Open, I'll have to convince the girls to do the real thing. You've got magic in your veins. That's what's important."

Suddenly, I felt faint again. How much wine had I really had? It felt like Tiberius had a heavy pouring paw. "Maybe I should lay down. This is all a little... much. In fact, I have to head back to the mainland tomorrow and arrange my flight home."

"But you haven't solved anything yet."

"Like what?"

"Anything! I could have been killed viciously in my sleep. Avenge me, girlie."

"I am not a girl!" I exploded, pain lashing behind my eyes. "I'm an overwhelmed forty-year old woman who has never had a proper vacation. I came here to recuperate after a shock. Not to become private investigator for a witch. Oh my God. I literally just said witch like it was normal. This isn't normal. Nothing is normal. I'm going crazy. I'm—"

The chipmunk slapped me across the face. "Snap out of it, Ava!"

I stared wide-eyed at the little creature. "I'm officially certifiable. Before I only considered the possibility, but now I know. Lock me up and throw away the key."

Nonna put her hands in a prayer position. "Please. You have to stay. I don't understand why the island let you in, but she did. There's a reason, we just have to uncover it, and my gut tells me it has to do with the ghosts."

"That does not sound healthy for me. In fact," I said, heading for my room to pack my bags, "that sounds like a one-way ticket to a horror film. No thanks. Great hospitality, I'll leave you a decent Yelp review."

Nonna's body went limp in her chair, her head lolling backwards. A cold chill spun across my skin. Candles sputtered out and a bookcase wobbled. "Nonna?" I inched closer. Her eyes were milky and unseeing.

Crap.

What if she was having a heart attack or a stroke? She was over a hundred, so the odds weren't in her favor. "I'm going to call 911. Wait, what's the Italian equivalent?" I asked the chipmunk.

Before he could respond, Nonna's lifeless body popped up, her face twisted and skeletal. Her mouth was a large vortex of blackness as she screamed Mummy-style at me in another astral projection.

I shrieked and stumbled back. "You can't scare me into staying," I said, rubbing my chest where my heart beat erratically from being completely, blindingly terrified. "Even if I wanted to, which I'm not saying I do, I can't. My horrible ex-husband apparently gambled our life savings away, and I have to go home to find a job. My money is gone. I have nothing."

Tiberius and Nonna glanced at each other. The chipmunk nodded.

"How do you like Italian winters?" Nonna asked cheerfully, back in her body. Like it wasn't the world's most leading question. Or like she hadn't accused me of murder an hour ago.

"Um."

"Great! We can forge the signatures on my will, and you can take over the B&B. There's plenty of money, even without tourism, so you'll be set."

"Why would we have to forge them? It's your will."

"Don't be ridiculous. We couldn't get a lawyer out here to make it official. They'd never get through the veil."

"What?"

"Oh, it's fine. There's nothing to forgery. My skill set used to be a hot commodity back in the war. Falsified passports, papers, money, you name it, I did it."

"Oh good, more lawbreaking," I muttered.

Tiberius hopped onto Nonna's shoulder and whispered in her ear. They both looked at me, and I heard Nonna whisper back, "Eh. Seems a little much."

Tiberius gave her a stern talking that I didn't understand. It didn't sound Italian or English.

"Fine!" Nonna exploded.

"Will somebody tell me what's going on?"

Nonna didn't meet my eyes. "If you're going to take over Villa Venus, there's one more housekeeping note. Aurick is definitely not human."

Chapter Seven

RUDELY, they didn't give me a minute to let that sink in. When I got home, I was doing it. I was going to be petty and give this place a one-star rating. Would not recommend. Not even if you were a witch in the making.

"And?" Tiberius prodded.

"It's not just Aurick," Nonna continued. "The whole town is supernatural."

"The whole town?" I sputtered, wine sloshing out of my glass and onto the antique table. I tried to nonchalantly wipe it away.

"Except for Luca," Nonna said hastily. "He came as a heart-broken tourist and never left. We didn't want to break his heart again and so we sort of…"

"Lied?" I offered dryly.

"Withheld information," Nonna corrected. "Magic mostly cloaks itself anyway. As long as the shifters don't get too shifty in front of him, he'll never know."

"And Aurick really is a…" I gulped, forcing the word out, but it deflated into a whisper. "Vampire?"

Nonna wheezed laughter. "No, no." She paused. "Actually, we're not quite sure what he is. Like you, he showed up one day through the veil. This island has its mysteries. He might not even be here anymore."

"Didn't you check on him yesterday?"

"To be honest, I forgot. And he's never been in town. I doubt anyone but us even knows he's here."

My stomach roiled at all of the news.

"One final thing, girlie."

What else could this old broad have to tell me? Spaceships would soon arrive to take us on an all-expense paid trip to Mars? Jim would magically give me all his money if I cursed him? On second thought, that didn't sound like the worst thing in the world.

"Make sure you plug your ears when coming and going. Thessaly likes to sunbathe on the rocks below."

"Who?"

"Thessaly, the siren."

"I'm sorry," I snorted. "I thought you said siren, like from a mythology book."

"She almost got you yesterday, but she's mostly harmless. All of the residents are."

Tiberius snorted. "That's an understatement. When's the last time a witch hexed anyone?"

"Accidentally or on purpose?" Nonna asked.

"If you have to ask, that's the problem," he replied tartly.

I opened my mouth to protest, but quickly closed it. Honestly, what did I have to go back to? The endless job search, where I would have to demean myself to a bunch of twenty-year-olds for minimum wage? Or finding an apartment on Craig's List without a serial killer roommate? Oh God, a roommate. While Jim had felt more like a roommate than a husband the past few years, I had a feeling it would be different with an actual stranger.

Even if this was a big con job, I didn't have anything to lose, and at least Aradia had beautiful views, an interesting history, ghosts, and wine. Lots of delicious Italian wine. And delicious Italian men. Luca's face wavered in front of my mind's eye. His salt and pepper hair—and saltier personality. I liked them dry. And tall. And delicious.

Nonna snapped me out of my musings. "Come on, girlie. Time to meet your destiny."

And you know what? I agreed to go with the midlife crisis flow.

"LET'S GO INTO TOWN. Even though it's past noon, I'm sure the two lazabouts are at Rosemary's Bakery, probably on their third espresso and biscotti. We'll have to convince them to do the ritual, but it shouldn't be hard. Just offer them something from the mainland. You brought presents, *si?*"

"Um..."

"Any old thing will do. We used to have a few brave souls cross the waters to bring us supplies, but that dried up over an... incident."

"Why does that sound like a vampire sucked all of your supplier's blood?"

"I haven't the faintest. A tube of lipstick will do. Rosemary has been bemoaning her dwindling supply."

By now, I was getting used to Nonna's ramblings. I nodded politely, going back to my room to fix my hair, put on some make-up, and stuff an extra tube of lipstick in my purse. For being a tiny town on an isolated island, the women and men always had their hair coiffed and faces done. Before, I thought it was an Italian thing. Now I wondered if it was a magic thing.

As we left, I dutifully plugged my ears with cotton balls, half-wondering if there truly was a siren living on the rocks below and half-wondering why Nonna didn't have to plug hers. Perhaps the siren didn't affect her on principle. Maybe they were friends or maybe Nonna threatened to hex her if she ever tried.

Or maybe, she didn't exist.

Tiberius claimed he had better things to do and scampered up a walnut tree. "Suit yourself," Nonna said, putting on her lime green helmet and motoring down the steep drive. I kicked my own Vespa into gear and followed, the whine of the motor reduced to a dull buzz.

The windy dirt road turned into cobblestones and the town came into view. All of the houses were made of beautiful wheaten-colored stones usually found in Rome. The towering buildings curved gently inwards, as if time pulled them together. It was truly a medieval city, and I couldn't help but love it—despite it apparently housing all sorts of supernatural creatures.

When I wasn't feeling crazy, I felt alive here for the first time in a long time. Confident. Like my old self was coming back. I didn't want all of it back, just the parts that mattered. My old courage and determination. I missed them, buried as they were under a suburban soccer mom shine. It had felt good at the time, but that life was gone, and I wanted to find the old me and merge it into the midlife me. The one who didn't go along with something because it was easy.

Nonna said there were only about a hundred inhabitants, and I felt a few heads swiveling to watch me as we entered the town. I had the feeling their curiosity was strong and their gossip game stronger. What would a human do that was out of the ordinary? Breathe through their nose? Did we have a particular scent? What if there really were vampires? I was the only mortal around besides Luca. What did they eat to survive?

My body shuddered and the moped wobbled. "Keep it together, Ava," I muttered, righting the handle bars and managing to stay on the road. Back in my teen days, I'd hot wired a motorcycle. Now I could barely handle a Vespa? Pathetic. I had turned into a house cat. Declawed and domesticated.

Nonna rounded a corner at breakneck speed and came to a halt in the square. In the light of day, I had a chance to see it clearly. Each side consisted of one building with narrow entrances between them. The baby cherub fountain was still cute during the day, and a few cats sunbathed lazily on stoops.

Rosemary's Bakery shared a wall with the taverna. The tables and chairs were still out, but the wine and tea lights were gone. For being the only bakery in town, it was empty.

I pulled out my cotton balls and glanced around. "Kind of quiet, don't you think?" I whispered.

It felt right in the moment, like the Renaissance ghost might sense my presence and pop out again. As much as I loved the idea of ghosts, I realized I didn't love them hitting on me.

"You're right, girlie. Let's investigate," Nonna said, putting a finger to the side of her nose. "Something doesn't smell right."

We cautiously walked up to the bakery and peered inside. The door was locked, and it appeared to have been abandoned in a hurry. A chair was overturned, and there were napkins and silverware scattered across the black and white tiled floor. A coffee cup dripped from where it had been knocked over, half-finished.

"How many violent crimes do you get on Aradia?" I whispered.

"None. I told you. The most Luca does is yell at Marco for home brewing absinthe that will singe your nose hairs off."

"Does he stop?"

"Hasn't yet." Nonna bobbed around to peer in the other window. "Maybe I should spell the lock open."

"Let me try." I pulled out a hair pin and inserted it into the tumblers. Carefully, I felt around until the ends snapped into place. The medieval door clicked and, with a soft whine, swung open.

"Full of secrets, aren't you, girlie?" Nonna patted me on the back and put a finger to her wizened lips. "Now, follow me and keep quiet."

I nodded, preparing myself for... something. What if the bakery was closed because of a magical attack? I doubted another witch or monster would be frightened off by my hair pin. Heck, I didn't even know what sort of monsters existed.

Nonna tiptoed through the wreckage, and I was impressed at her catlike ability. On the other hand, she probably weighed ninety pounds dripping wet.

She stopped and put an arm out to catch me. "I hear something."

I strained to listen, and then I heard it too. Grunting. Something big was in the back room. Something big and animalistic.

I needed a better weapon. Frantically, I grabbed the broken espresso cup and nodded for Nonna to proceed. What had my life come to that I had to brandish a weapon twice in one morning?

The grunting got louder. It sounded almost like a predator growling. Nonna pressed two fingers to her side and did another complicated gesture, like I was supposed to understand spy talk. I made a mental note to ask later if she was part of the Resistance during WWII.

She held up three fingers, then two. On one, she flung open the door, already chanting something ancient. Multiple people screamed, including me. Inside, a large, hairy and very stunned lion was morphing into a human, his humanoid butt still covered in golden hair.

The woman below him looked normal and un-eaten. She also looked mad. "Nonna," she yelled. "How many times have I told you to knock before you enter!"

It appears, for the second time in a week, I'd walked in on people doing the down and dirty.

Chapter Eight

"HAVE YOU NO SHAME?" the woman screeched at Nonna who was still watching as the lion-man yanked up his pants and buckled them. I was fairly certain it was Marco, but I really, really did not want to know. The woman, I guessed, was Rosemary.

Her curls were messy, as if someone had been running their claws through them, and her face flushed. "I'm so sorry. We'll just—"

Nonna cackled, interrupting my rambling. "Marco, you old dog. I'm sorry, I mean cat."

Rosemary straightened her half-buttoned baker's outfit. "It's fine. I need to open for the lunch, as do you, *caro mio*." She gave Marco a kiss on the cheek.

Marco roared and huffed, clearly not happy about this turn of events, but Rosemary took his elbow and led him out of the storage room. "How about a cuppa before you go, my love? Sit over there."

Sheepishly, we righted the tables and chairs and cleaned up the coffee cups. If I were a betting type, I'd say

Marco half-shifted into a lion as he chased Rosemary into the back room for some midday pleasure.

"Rosemary and Marco have been together for decades now. Right?" Nonna called.

Rosemary bustled behind the marble counter, pouring us beautifully thick shots of espresso. "*Sì*. We found each other on the island in our time of need. Aradia is special that way."

She came over with a gilt tray of cups and saucers and petite orders of biscotti, which she set in front of us. "They're hazelnut chocolate. Dunk it first on this end, please. No, no, all wrong! This way, darling."

Marco grunted, "Don't mind Rosemary, she's a harpy. She'll nag you all day long, and she's quite particular about her baked goods."

Before I knew what I was doing, I leapt from the table, totally ignoring the fact that I didn't know these people or that one of them was part lion, and smacked Marco over the head with my purse full of goodies. "No woman is a harpy," I growled through gritted teeth, my chest heaving. Triggered.

Marco bristled. Golden fur teemed to life on his skin, rapidly covering his body and crawling up his face in long, thick clumps. His teeth, too, expanded, growing to the length of my forefinger before Rosemary burst out laughing.

She gave him a kiss on his curled, snarling lips. "*Dio Mio*, Marco, we're getting a divorce so I can marry Ava."

Marco's fur receded quicker than my ex's hairline, and he smoothed back the hair on his head like nothing extraordinary had happened, although he did give me a last glare before going to open up the taverna.

"Darling, I am a harpy. It's my nature," Rosemary

explained. She paused. "You are a supernatural, right? How else would you have gotten inside the veil?"

My face must have reflected how faint I felt. Nonna jumped in smoothly. "We're not sure. Something, obviously. Aradia doesn't make mistakes. Besides Luca, but he doesn't count. Aradia clearly knew he needed us."

I could barely get past the part where they acted like the island had a consciousness, so I ignored that bit for now. "I'm so sorry. I can't believe I clocked your husband. Shall I just pack my things and apologize on my way out or do you need to exact some sort of public shaming first? I saw a pillory post on my way into town."

Rosemary patted my hand and gave me another biscotti while Nonna almost choked she was laughing so hard. I was glad I was such a delight to her.

"Don't worry about it. You're not the first to give him a good smack. You probably won't be the last."

Still, I was mortified.

"What you need," Rosemary said, "is a proper girls' night out with women your own age. Nonna is great and all, but…"

"Watch your tongue, girlie," Nonna pointed a chocolate-covered biscotti at her. Good to know I wasn't the only one she considered a girlie.

"…you should enjoy all that Aradia has to offer," Rosemary finished firmly. "I'll call Coronis and we'll meet you at the taverna around eight p.m.?"

"That sounds amazing, but I can't stay. I'm about to go through what will presumably be a very messy divorce, which means I need to find a job in the States. This trip was just a midlife crisis weekend fling."

"Ah. I'm sorry," Rosemary said, her glossy ringlets bouncing in sympathy. "Sometimes those we love the most hurt us the easiest." From the way her eyes darkened, I got the feeling she knew from experience.

"Like when Marco bit you last year and I had to stitch the hole in your ass? I hope that was worth it," Nonna chortled.

"Quiet, you. And yes, it was worth it."

"I don't think my marriage included true love," I said thoughtfully. "I mean, I appreciated my ex for what he did for me, but he barely had the power to truly wound me. It was more my pride than my heart that hurt when I found him sleeping with my assistant. Wow! You're the first people I've told that to. Not even my sons know."

"Sons?" Nonna looked up sharply. "You already have children?"

"Yes, I'm not the young girlie you think. I've raised twin boys!"

"What a feat," Rosemary laughed with me. "I've no children of my own, but I've seen enough of these hellions to know I'm quite okay without one. I'm sure yours, however, are perfectly behaved."

"Not in the slightest," I assured her. "That last year of high school is like the last month of pregnancy. You just want them out, out, out!"

It was easy and comfortable talking to her. Unlike Nonna who was starting to make me paranoid. I couldn't believe we broke into a perfectly fine bakery on a gut feeling. She probably still believed I murdered her this morning.

"A feat," Nonna echoed softly. She snapped out of whatever reverie she was in and drained her cup. "Come on, Ava. I'm going to show you exactly why you can stay another night and, frankly, as many nights as you want."

Rosemary rolled her eyes, but she had to handle more customers looking for a midday pick-me-up. "Good luck!"

she waved to me as we left. "Hopefully, I'll see you tonight!"

I waved back, following Nonna to our Vespas. Was it really that easy to make friends? It always felt so difficult back home, more like a chore than anything else. Even when I had the boys it wasn't easy. I had to stake out the playground and determine which moms were my type. There was a fine line between being too put together and too frazzled, and I never found the right balance. School kids didn't know how easy they had it. All they had to do was figure out who dressed like them, or liked the same music, or needed to study for that impossible chemistry test and bam—instant friendship.

"Get ready for some rough riding, Mamma," Nonna shouted over her shoulder.

The change in my pet name jolted me. "What did you call me?"

"You've graduated. Enjoy it, Mamma. Now, focus on the road. This old island is wily."

Before I could protest that it was just an island, a sinkhole opened a few feet in front of me. I swerved and almost nailed an errant goat. As he bleated indignantly, I tumbled off, my Vespa rolling a few more feet before crashing on its side. I yelped and rolled, holding my arm.

"Mamma!" Nonna raised a fist, yelling obscenities at the island before circling back to check on me. "Just a scrape," she murmured. "There now. Easy does it."

I held my battered arm, but it didn't appear to be broken. I'd done that once before at our company's co-ed softball game after attempting to steal home. I went straight from third to the hospital, but I've always been competitive. The minute they discharged me, I ran straight back to the field. Another team was playing, and they were quite confused by the hollering middle-aged woman stomping on home plate.

"Can you still ride?"

I nodded, feeling a little shaky at my brush with a serious accident on a foreign island with no hospital. I didn't even know if they had a doctor. Plus, the way that sinkhole had appeared reminded me of the earthquake back home. Like it was meant for me. Before, that would have seemed ridiculous. Now... I wasn't sure. "Where did that come from? One minute, the road was fine..."

Nonna helped me up, dusting off my jeans and speckled blouse. She narrowed her eyes at the road. "Keep it together. We're not here to kill anyone today, you old she-devil."

"Excuse me?"

Nonna hopped back on her Vespa. "Keep your eyes peeled. Aradia still fancies herself wild."

"The island?"

"Of course, girlie! I mean, Mamma."

"Just clarifying," I muttered.

"Hurry now. You want to make apertivo hour with the other girls, don't you?"

Nonna was right. I absolutely wanted to make one last apertivo hour before I had to stumble home and find a new life.

"The graveyard is to the left over this hill," Nonna shouted.

"The what?" I screeched, but Nonna either didn't hear me or was ignoring me. I'd bet a round of Botox it was the latter.

After we crested the hill, the cypress trees grew closer together in gnarled clumps, casting the road in dark shadows. Despite it being early in the afternoon, a chill settled over the land.

Before, this would have been the highlight of my trip. Now, I prayed we didn't meet anything else in the cemetery. Which was literally the first time I hoped *not* to see a ghost in my life.

The dirt road came to an end in a thicket of trees and plants, and Nonna signaled for us to get off and continue on foot.

"Is everyone from the island buried here?" I whispered. It felt wrong to talk too loud.

"No one has been interred for hundreds of years. Then again, no one has died, either."

I lurched at her words. "What do you mean no one has died?"

Like usual, Nonna ignored me and crept over twisted vines, going deeper into the grove. It was surrounded by crumbling fluted columns and ancient arches. I half-expected my Renaissance wannabe lover to poke his lacy ruff out and yell, "Boo!"

As she walked, Nonna tapped random urns and muttered to herself. The urns looked ancient, like old Roman vases. Some had intricate scrollwork. Others showcased beautiful women at their toilette, servants pinning up their hair or buffing their makeup.

From the inscriptions I could decipher on the older headstones, this burial ground was founded in 1220. They must have re-used the Roman urns, and I wondered if they dumped out the previous occupant before filling it with the cremated remains of the freshly departed.

"Wait, how old are Marco and Rosemary?"

"Does it matter?"

"Maybe."

Nonna shrugged. "Hard to say. Now help me dig. My bones are older than the ones in this cemetery," she cackled.

I honestly couldn't tell if she was joking or not, so I decided not to pry. It seemed easier that way.

We were in a slightly newer part of the cemetery, meaning the tombstones were from the fifteen-hundreds and had witty little sayings like *Towards Immortality*, and my personal favorite, *She possessed a fondness for the finer things in life*. And let my headstone read: *She enjoyed wine*.

Nonna handed me a stick and marked an X next to one of the smaller, less ornate urns. "Dig here and be precise. You might not like what you find if you go wandering."

With that, I began digging exactly where she pointed.

As she waited, Nonna walked circles around me, crunching over fallen twigs and leaves, her long, silk robe rustling with each step. "Hurry up, Mamma. I smell something coming."

"Smell?"

"Don't you? It's sulfuric with a hint of tomato and something else. Maybe... oregano?"

"No. I'm absolutely not getting the same smells you are." In fact, it smelled like a wet graveyard with decaying leaves and a lack of sunlight. Except it was almost two p.m. in southern Italy.

Nonna froze.

"Are you okay?" I asked.

She put a finger to her lips as a now-familiar chill swept over me. A cold wind curled around my face, without rustling any of the leaves on the trees or Nonna's dress.

A ghost wind.

Chapter Nine

"GET BEHIND ME," Nonna ordered.

"You're a 115 years old. Shouldn't you get behind me?"

"And let you get killed? I don't think so. The island's attempt today was merely a warning shot. She will grow more determined."

"You're saying the island is alive. Not just plants and birds, but the actual island?"

"Get behind me," Nonna replied. Her voice was short but firm.

Never one to take direction well, I stood next to her studying the grove. I could have sworn I saw moonlight drift across the urns, but then it solidified.

"Orbs," I whispered.

"*Sì.*"

"Can they manifest?"

"*Certo che sì!*"

"Okay, okay. So what do we do? And why do they keep showing up?"

"We'll have to ask Tiberius later. If we survive."

There was a high-pitched wail, the kind only centipedes or some other invertebrate could've understood, and then the glowing orbs began to race around the cemetery. I could have sworn they were attacking... each other?

"Watch out!" I yelled, diving out of the way as the orbs launched themselves into the air.

During the tussle, they began to take shape—a man and a woman with their ghostly hands around each other's necks. They were shouting in Italian, but I didn't need a translator to get the gist.

"Should we do something?" I asked Nonna.

"No. It's too dangerous. Ghosts can be very unpredictable. Dig fast and let's get out of here."

I was about to follow her lead when the ghosts spotted me. I froze.

The translucent woman wore a long, tattered gown that once had red and white stripes. A few whalebones from her corset poked through the fabric, as if they were her own ribs sticking out. "You must help me. I want to move on." She held out her arms and floated closer, beseeching me, but her combatant, a man in full metal armor and a chainmail headpiece butted his way in front.

"*Sì*, I want her to move on, too. I am sick and tired of listening to her whine about her husband." The knight bounced up and down. "It's been hundreds of years. Time to get a new hobby."

"He drowned me in my own tomato sauce!" she exclaimed.

"Did you ever stop to think you deserved it?"

"I swear, one of these days, I will figure out how to throw away one of your bones, and you'll have to fetch it from the cliff like the dog that you are," the woman threatened. I could tell she was just warming up, so I took a chance and stepped between them. Their insults were locked and loaded after centuries of arguing. Or, you know, like any couple married for longer than ten years.

"Stop!" I shouted. "I'm not from here. I have no idea how to help you."

"Go on. Get back," Nonna said, fumbling with an evil eye amulet at her neck. The ghosts ignored her. I had the feeling they'd been doing this song and dance for many lifetimes, and nothing, not even a spelled amulet, was going to change that.

They finally separated, the man breathing heavily through his full suit of armor. "It was that siren. She lured me over the cliff and drowned me in the ocean. Then she ate the flesh off my bones. Help me first."

"That's a lie. You did not drown in the ocean, and she did not eat your flesh! I can see it and smell it hanging off of you now! I am the most deserving. Tomato sauce! Can you imagine how thick and chunky it is to drown in tomato sauce? A piece of oregano got caught in my nostril, and it burned like actual hell."

"You haven't had a chance to get to hell yet, although you've certainly made this afterlife feel like one," the knight snapped.

"*Attento a come parli,*" she snarled. *Watch your mouth.*

"*Sta' zitto!*"

"Everyone, quiet!" I put two fingers to my lips and let out a long dog whistle. It sounded like nails on a chalkboard, and the ghosts covered their ears and howled. "I have no idea why you think I can help you move on, but have you ever considered that you don't want to?" I asked. "How many years—no centuries—has it been?"

They both started arguing once again, so I let out another ear-splitting whistle. "No arguing! Both of you sit."

They immediately sat cross-legged and hovered over the graves.

"That's better." I began to pace in front them, my arms behind my back. "I'm going to ask you questions one at a time. Got it?"

They nodded.

"Good. Okay, you." I pointed to the woman. "When did you pass away?"

"Murdered. When was I murdered by my no good louse of a husband? 1685."

"Any unfinished business? I mean, your husband is already long gone." Good Lord, I couldn't believe I was asking a ghost from the seventeenth century for their unfinished business, like I was somehow going to fix it.

She lifted her shoulders dramatically. "How should I know? It's been a long time. What I do know is that I'm still angry."

"Understandably so," I said soothingly. "And you?" I nodded at the Knight.

He stuck out his chest. "I was killed in the Year of our Lord, Fifteen Hundred and Forty whilst fighting for the Holy Land."

I racked my brain. "Was that a crusade year?"

The knight creaked a bit while the woman burst out laughing. "Ha! He claims the siren got him, but he fell off his horse on the journey to the Holy Land and drowned in two inches of water because he was too fat to roll over in his armor and get his nose out of the mud."

"I hate myself for knowing you," he muttered.

"Not as much as I hate you," she responded.

I held up my hands, feeling like a referee by this point. "Did you ever stop to think that you don't want to move on, not because you're afraid of what's on the other side, nor because you have unfinished business, but because you'll miss each other?"

The two gaped at me while Nonna chuckled somewhere off to my left.

"Well I never," the woman finally said. "The very idea that I would even harbor one feeling that wasn't complete antipathy for this, this—"

"Robust, manly, Knight of St. John, the Hospitaller Order?" he interrupted smugly.

"*Chi ti credi di essere?*" she shrieked. *Who do you think you are?*

"The man of your dreams apparently," he responded.

While they bickered, Nonna waved me over to where she'd been digging. "It's down there, Mamma."

"What is?" My voice was barely above a butterfly's flutter.

"Everything you'll need to stay here for as long as you want."

"I thought Aradia was trying to kill me."

"Well, sure. But she rarely succeeds."

"Nonna, sometimes I think you're being serious." Ghosts were one thing. I'd always wanted to believe in them, but an island with a consciousness that was trying to kill me? Right.

She patted my cheek and then turned my chin to where she'd opened a chest-sized hole in the ground.

"Jackpot," I whispered.

Chapter Ten

THIS TIME, I didn't need a doctor to diagnose me. I had gold fever. My mouth was dry and my tongue fuzzy as I gaped at the literal buried treasure beneath me. Then reason butted its way into my consciousness. "Why do you have ancient Roman treasure buried in a graveyard?"

"Why wouldn't I? One never knows when a rainy day may come."

"Right. Silly me."

She pointed out the silver and gold bars of precious metals. "Those are ingots that I liberated from a passing merchant ship."

"You mean a shipwreck?"

"They hardly needed them, those thieves."

"Because their ship had sank and they were dead?"

"Sure."

I shot her a scowl, but she was too busy digging around for something else to notice. The woman probably had a century's worth of junk buried down there. Hoarding: Extreme *Strega* Edition.

"What about those ghosts? Should we help them? Do you have any spells?"

Nonna wiped some sweat out of her eyes and leaned against an urn. "I think you've showed them the light they were looking for. While it may not be *the* light, it is the light they needed to see."

"You think?" I glanced over at the odd couple as they began gesticulating wildly.

"I do. Help me lift a few of these ingots into my bag."

"Why do you need them here on Aradia?" I asked, heaving under the weight of pure gold. "It seems like everyone sort of looks out for each other."

"We do. Like I said, they're for a rainy day. In this case, the best American lawyer ingots can buy. You're the most interesting thing to happen to this island in a long time, and I'm not ready to give you up yet."

My heart swelled. "Aw, thanks, Nonna. You've grown on me, too. You know, in the twenty-four hours I've known you. So is Luca the only one who pays for things?"

"Yeah, it makes him feel better to pay in Euros, so we let him."

After we covered up the remaining gold, we tiptoed out of the graveyard so the ghosts wouldn't see us leaving and rode back to Villa Venus. As soon as we left the circle of gnarled trees, the sun beat down as before and the air cleared of its dank, brimstone smell. Aradia even left me alone—if Nonna was to be believed.

At this point, I wasn't quite sure what to think. As a child, strange things happened around me all the time, which was probably why I didn't last long with foster families or why the streets never bothered me. Feral dogs and rabid coyotes always appeared to spook away any would-be bullies.

"Are you going into town with me tonight?" I asked as we lugged the ingots inside.

"No, Mamma. You enjoy yourself with the other girlies."

"Are you sure? I could bring you back something to eat."

Nonna squeezed my hands, her grip surprisingly strong. Her hands were ice, probably from poor circulation. I should tell her about the red algae supplement I'd read about.

"I'll be fine. Thank you, Mamma."

I went back and drew a bath in the clawfoot tub. It was in the shared bathroom across the hall, but Aurick never came out of his room, so I felt fine indulging in a deep soak with lavender buds and a book I'd plucked off the shelf. I couldn't remember when I'd last had time for a bath.

As I lay in the water, my toes peeking over the bubbles, I began to remember why. Baths were the worst. And the book turned out to be an unabridged copy of the *Aeneid*. I couldn't say it was riveting, but I guess it helped capture the ambiance of ancient Rome. I skipped to the middle where Aeneas meets Queen Dido. Maybe it would pick up.

While I read, I kept wondering how long I had to stay in the water to feel relaxed. Twenty minutes? Thirty? I checked the clock by the sink. Eh. Fifteen was fine. Maybe I'd try a glass of rosé next time to see if that helped.

I put the book back on the shelf, a bad taste in my mouth from the one chapter I'd managed to read. Poor Dido. Despite being the queen of Carthage, she was forced by the gods to fall in love with Aeneas. Then, thanks to the gods, she was betrayed by Aeneas, and she fell on his sword. Where's the justice in that? And he had the balls to approach her in the underworld. For what? Forgiveness? I cheered a little when she refused to look at him. That was quite enough of that book.

Clearly, if I was ever going to get back into the dating pool, I'd have to work some things out. When I paid special attention to my hair and makeup today, I did it for me. The leopard-print dress I'd picked out, the one that showed off my curves—also for me. For now, that would be my new focus. Me.

I gave my lips a few last smacks as I checked all the angles. A few stray chin hairs had had the audacity to begin popping up lately, like they thought my eyesight was so bad I wouldn't notice.

I noticed.

I plucked them and misted on my make-up setting spray so the wind and bugs wouldn't mess things up too much. On my way through the kitchen, I asked Nonna one last time if she wanted to go.

"Don't worry about me. I'll be fine with Tiberius."

The chipmunk gave me a salute from inside the walnut bowl, and I vowed not to eat any walnuts from it ever again.

"Okay, if you're sure," I said slowly.

She shooed me out. "Go, have fun. Get to know the girlies. Eat some of Marco's cooking. You'll never want to leave."

"I knew this was all a ploy to get me to take over the villa."

Nonna chucked me under the chin. "You're the smart one."

I took the spare Vespa and promised myself only two glasses of wine. Whether or not there truly was an ancient creature waiting to lure me to my death, the cliffs were not safe at night.

The ride to town was quaint, and the sea made a lovely

soundtrack. I never understood why the younger generation had to go around with headphones for a simple commute to the city. Especially young girls. Being a woman made it painfully clear we needed our senses about us at all times, and that was the sad truth.

Rosemary met me in front of Marco's taverna, no trace of embarrassment on her face after we'd barged in on her afternoon delight. She greeted me with open arms, and her embrace smelled like yeast and sweet dough. I adored her instantly. She wore a lacy navy-blue dress, and I had a feeling she dressed that way all of the time. Italian fashion plate for the forty-plus crowd. A little different from my own leopard print dress.

"*Ciao*, darling," she said, kissing me on both cheeks. "I'm so glad you made it. Come, sit. Marco will bring us some fabulous wine, and we'll get to know each other. It's not every day a new woman comes to Aradia!"

"I brought gifts," I said. "Nonna mentioned you haven't been getting any shipments of lipstick lately?"

Rosemary dove into the bag. "Oh, you are too good!"

Marco banged open the wooden door and sat down two glasses of thick, delicious looking red wine. "An Aradia specialty," he announced.

We swirled and sniffed, finally clinking before our first sip. "Oh wow! I taste blackberries and chocolate." I sniffed again and took another sip. "Maybe something like… leather?"

Marco nodded in acknowledgment of my appreciation. "That's the medium body. I'll get your nibbles, *cara mia*."

As they kissed, perhaps a little more passionately than would be considered polite in front of virtual strangers, another woman I hadn't met yet walked up to join our table. Marco pulled away, smiling at his wife. Rosemary stood and I quickly followed suit to exchange customary greetings.

If I thought Rosemary was fashionable, this woman embodied the very ideal. She wore a long black velvet skirt with slits up both sides. She had knotted a red and white polka dot halter top at her navel and tied a matching silk scarf around her neck. Her bobbed hair was ice white, which contrasted with her clear blue eyes. "*Ciao*, darling," she said, casually draping herself in the next chair. I even saw tattoos swirling up the back of her arms and a few under her halter.

"Coronis, meet Ava Falcetti. She's visiting from America and completely adorable. Look what she brought us!"

The woman turned her head, as if observing me from another viewpoint. "Is she now? What brings you here?"

"Midlife crisis," I said casually. "I've always wanted to travel, and Italy pretty much was my list."

"As it should be," Coronis said. "Italy is the best place to drown one's sorrows. *Riempi il bicchiere quando è vuoto, vuota il bicchiere quando è pieno.* It's an Italian proverb and one of my favorite ones."

"It's beautiful. What does it mean?"

"Fill your glass when empty, empty your glass when full." Coronis clinked my wine glass.

After the cheers, I swirled the red liquid gold in my cup, considering if it was okay to ask what sort of supernatural being she was. On the one hand, I was dying to know. On the other hand, I didn't want to actually die by asking a supernatural a socially unacceptable question.

Rosemary sensed my curiosity. "How you are getting along in this wild town?"

"It's been interesting. I'm still absorbing." I didn't know

if I should mention the second ghost encounter or the secret cache of ingots, so I didn't.

"Coronis is one of our more special residents. You came here when? Remind me, darling."

"Oh, that. I can't quite recall. But it was after Alfred's little film."

"Alfred?"

"Hitchcock, darling," Rosemary said. "Coronis used to be a movie star, just like Nonna. We have an affinity for golden era film stars in Italy."

"Have you ever seen that 1960s photograph of Tippi Hedren and a crow?" Coronis asked, lighting a long, tapered cigarette and leaning back. "It was a promotional image for his film, *The Birds*."

"The one where the crow is holding a lit match and lighting a cigarette dangling from Tippi's mouth?"

"That's the one."

"Are you going to tell me you're Tippi Hedren, even though she's alive and well in the States?"

"Oh, you are adorable," Coronis said.

Rosemary nodded. "I told you. Adorable."

Coronis laughed. "No, of course not. I'm the crow."

My wine went down a little scratchy as I covered up a cough of shock. "Excuse me?"

"Would you like to see?" Coronis took my open mouth as an affirmative. With a graceful twirl, she leapt into the air, glossy black feathers cascading down her back as she grew to the size of an energy efficient, compact car. It was the complete opposite of her ice queen hair and eyes.

"Whoa," I breathed.

Coronis cawed a few times, strutting in her form. Her beak snapped in the air, and I had shivers up and down my body at the power of her jaw.

Before, I could sort of brush aside the crazy with a list

of potential causes. Dreams, lack of sleep, jet lag. Did I really see a talking chipmunk and Nonna floating in an astral projection? No, of course not! But when the crazy kept happening, it got harder to explain. And let's be honest, I didn't want to anyway.

"Do you have a minute to talk about our lord and savior, Edgar Allen Poe?" I asked teasingly. At their blank stares, I tried to pull up a picture of the meme, but still no WIFI. "Hm, no internet, but there's a funny picture of a crow walking next to a cat who has the most annoyed look on his face and that quote on it. A personal favorite of mine."

Coronis snapped her beak, a little more ferociously than before.

"But probably not a joking matter," I added hastily. "Does Luca ever notice anything odd?" I asked as she slipped gracefully back into a woman. Coronis puckered her lips and applied a brilliant ruby red.

"You both are what we call MILF's," Rosemary said. "Most of your type go out of your way to ignore the obvious."

"Wait, is that why Nonna keeps calling me Mamma?"

The women cocked their heads, confused.

"MILF in America stands for..." I reddened, then scooted my chair closer and dropped my voice. "Mother I'd like to..." I trailed off, unsure of Italian polite society protocols.

"*Cosa?*" they begged. What?

"Mother I'd like to fuck," I said, my voice barely at a whisper now.

The two of them jerked back, roaring with laughter. I didn't see the joke, unless it was on me. My fingers got tingly, and I felt the same raw energy when Jim said something passive-aggressive.

"No, no. MILF stands for *Maevii Igneus Laceratrix Faex*. It's Latin and not exactly nice," Rosemary said.

"Basically, it refers to non-magical folks as wretched, life-draining dregs on society," Coronis added.

"Wait, I think Tiberius said that to me, but I was in no state of mind to follow a chipmunk's train of thought."

They nodded, understanding completely, and just like that the anxiety ebbed away. I couldn't articulate how wonderful it felt to be understood.

"Tiberius is a good influence on that old *strega*," Coronis said. "So, Ava Falcetti, a MILF in all manners," she continued with a wink, "What are your plans? It's nice having someone new on this old island."

I lifted my shoulders, taking another sip of the delicious wine. "I don't know. Nonna wants me to stay, but she thinks I'm a witch. She wants me to take over Villa Venus for some reason, but I barely know her."

"Are you?" they asked, in unison again.

"What? Taking over the villa?"

"A witch?" The women watched me closely.

"Absolutely not. I used to pretend I was back in my *Charmed* days, but nothing ever came of it. I couldn't even find enough girls to have a proper ritual. Then, I morphed that interest into ghost hunting. My husband thought it was stupid though, and well, I wanted to impress him. I wanted to be cool or normal or whatever, so I sort of stopped. Until I came here, the most supernatural my life got was when I watched re-runs of *Supernatural*."

"Eh? What's this?"

"An American television show. I watched it mostly for the sexy factor of the two male leads."

They nodded knowingly. I wondered what they did all day without any internet or telephone service. Aradia felt like an island lost to time. But the wine hadn't loosened my lips enough yet, and I felt too shy to ask. Instead, I said, "So Nonna really is a *strega*?"

"Nonna dabbles," Rosemary clarified. "She mostly arranges marriages for supernaturals offshore. A few healing potions, perhaps something a little darker from time to time if she's pissed. Mostly she clears up acne or gives it. Depending on her mood."

Coronis chimed in. "It's the old religion. *La Vecchia Religione*. A few hundred years ago, she would have been denounced as a *strega* and burned for her troubles."

"And now?"

"Now she's just Nonna," Coronis shrugged, sitting back to sip the rest of her espresso martini. "She's always trying to rope us into her schemes. We like life quiet. It's why we came here. We're not even proper witches! You have to be born into that sort of thing, like Nonna. We're halflings. Shifters can't ever be properly whole. Destined to be half-animal, half-human, we're doomed to live half-lives. The only powerful part-shifter here is Marco."

"I object to that!" Rosemary said indignantly. "We live a great life. Even if you're a shifter and I'm a harpy."

Right as I was about to ask what Marco was if it wasn't a full lion shifter, he arrived carrying a tray over his head that was probably as wide as I was tall. It smelled fantastic —of spices and cheese, fresh herbs, and pasta. There were prosciutto-wrapped dates stuffed with almonds and hard Italian cheeses, and more of his marinated bruschetta. He sat the tray on the empty table next to us and gave his wife another deep kiss.

"*Cara mia*," he said fondly, cupping her chin with his paw of a hand. She giggled like a school girl at his attention. "Ladies," he clapped his hands with gusto, that Italian spirit flowing through him. "I've brought you fresh zucchini salad, colatura risotto with ginger, and wild boar Bolognese. Ah, I forgot the melon and prosciutto."

"Don't worry about it. We'll have the melon tomorrow," Rosemary said. Then she turned to me, "You'll be staying, of course?"

"At this rate, I don't know how I couldn't," I admitted, picturing the ingots that could buy my way out of any trouble. Everything I'd done the last twenty years of my life —half of it!—was for others. Children's needs always came first, and the only "me time" I got was when Jim graciously watched the boys so I could run errands alone. Or finish the chores without the twins slipping frogs in my pockets and leaving mud pies on my counters.

Staying on an Italian island for an indefinite amount of time? Well, that would be just for me.

"Time enough to decide tomorrow. Now eat!" Rosemary invited. "That way we can drink more."

"I do love Bolognese," I gushed. "But I don't know what colatura is?"

"Basically, it's an Italian fish sauce," Coronis said, loading her plate with the risotto. "It's made with anchovies and salt, and left to age for up to three years. It's magnificent. I believe it's similar to the ancient Romans' garum sauce that they poured on everything."

"Try it," Rosemary urged at the apprehensive look on my face.

I scooped up a bite of the risotto and brought it eye level. "When in Rome, right?"

"When in Aradia," they sang together.

At first, I tasted only a briny saltiness. Then, the flavors exploded on my tongue, singing together with the ginger and garlic. It was such a wonderful mashup of coastal Southeast Asia and coastal Italy that I was lost in ecstasy for a moment. "Is this why you married Marco?"

"For his cooking?" Rosemary raised an eyebrow. "Certainly not."

Coronis giggled and let out a moan when she took a bite. "You're still not interested in a harem situation? A throuple? I promise to clean up after I molt."

"Molting. How sexy."

"Doing dishes. Sweeping. Even sexier," Coronis countered. She lowered her voice seductively. "Taking out the trash. Scrubbing. The. Oven."

"Oh, now you're speaking my love language."

They continued to gently rib each other while I soaked in this new Italian life. Hand gestures, loud aggressive voices, multiple instances of screaming, "*Stai scherzando?*" which I think meant, "Are you kidding me?" was a bit of a culture shock for someone like me who never made it out of the Midwest. I cherished every minute.

I leaned back, my plate clean and my heart full, content to watch the moonlight over the town square and swirl my funky wine. To be honest, I was quite sure I'd never had this before. Women joining forces for good rarely seemed to happen in my town. We were constantly keeping up appearances with and against each other.

Rosemary saw the smile at my lips. "What is it, darling? Do you want dessert?"

"Always," I grinned back.

A bottle later, I knew it was time to call it. "Well, ladies, it's been amazing, but I'm going to take my buzz home with me and dream of Italian late summer nights. I'll never forget you." I shot a fake finger gun at Coronis. "That's a cool party trick, crow-lady."

Okay, I was swaying. The wine seemed strong on Aradia. I wondered giddily if it was magical. Bottled under the light of a harvest moon or something like that.

Rosemary stood up, alarmed. "What do you mean? You've decided to go home?"

I struggled with the lime green helmet, thinking this was the time Luca needed to finally step in and arrest me. Handcuffs. Luca. Mmmm. I giggled, still struggling.

"It seems too easy. Like I haven't worked hard enough to deserve all of this." I waved the still-locked helmet at the town square. "It's too beautiful, too much, too... you know."

"Darling, we don't. It's just home. It can be your home. I can always use a set of hands at the bakery. As long as you like early mornings. I can't pay you a salary, but you'll never have to worry about food. Between Marco and I, we'll keep you fed."

"Whoa. Am I seeing ghosts or are you going blinky?" I flashed my hands open and closed.

"Another ghost?" Rosemary turned in her chair, bobbing her head to find it. A moment later, my Renaissance stalker wavered to life as he pretended to lounge idly in my chair, like he'd been there all along.

"You!" I pointed.

"*Scusi?*"

"Don't act like you don't know. Why are you so obsessed with me?"

Rosemary and Coronis watched agape. For being creatures of legend, I got the feeling ghosts were new to them.

The ghost soared into the air and produced a bouquet of wilted flowers. "I am but a romantic type, milady."

I couldn't help it. I snorted. "I'm the least ladylike person in the world."

"Maybe that's how I like my ladies."

"Ew."

The ghost got to his feet, which hovered six inches above the ground. "Before I was shocked by your presence.

Let me introduce myself as a proper gentleman. I am Piero Rossi, at your service." He flourished a bow. "One-time counselor to the great Medici family, now shipwrecked here. I've come to ask if you would do me the honor of dinner one night?"

I glanced around, practically begging for help. Rosemary and Coronis had their mouths covered with their hands, trying not to laugh. They gave me a thumbs up.

"You know, I just left my husband, and I'm more in the male maiming stage of grief than the revenge sex stage."

Somehow, that perked him up. "*Perfecto*! I don't have a male member you could harm."

At the look of abject horror on my face, he backtracked. "I'm sure I could figure out how to inhabit something though, when the time came. Tell me, how do you feel about sheep?"

The world was spinning by this point. "Not good, Piero. Not good."

Suddenly, Piero flickered. He looked as surprised as we did as he winked out.

"Piero?"

He appeared again, his pencil thin goatee shuddering as he solidified. "*Dio mio*, that was new."

"It was?" Rosemary asked.

"*Sì*." Piero looked shaken for a moment, but he quickly recovered. "Beautiful woman, I am pleading with you. One date. I will make it a night you will never forget."

"If I don't die."

"I would never kill you!"

"On purpose."

"Stop that!" Piero demanded. "I am true and trustworthy. Just ask the Medicis."

"Weren't they bloodthirsty tyrants who lied, cheated, and stole?"

Piero waved away my accusations like smoke. "Simply misunderstood."

"I'm sorry, Piero, but I'm not interested in a dead relationship. I'm sure you'll find a lovely ghost in the cemeteries of Aradia."

"Milady—"

"I said no!"

Piero flickered again, this time out of fear. Of me. Like I had done something to make him flicker. With a reproachful look, he vanished into smoke. I let out a breath, thankful that the ordeal was over. "Don't say anything," I pointed to the women who were going purple holding back their laughter.

"Oh darling, promise that you'll stay on Aradia!" Rosemary exclaimed. "You've really sparked this place to life."

A noise behind me made me pause. For a second, I thought Piero had nursed his broken heart in record time and decided to try again.

Worse. It was Luca. And I was officially seeing two of him.

Chapter Eleven

MY FACE flushed as Luca eyed me suspiciously. "You weren't planning to do what it looks like, correct?"

I pointed in both of his general directions. "You know, you have a weird accent. And you don't speak much Italian. In fact, everyone's English is perfect."

Luca raised an eyebrow. A manly eyebrow. A manly, bushy eyebrow. I bet he had a lot of chest hair. Jim didn't have any. Well, that wasn't true. He had three single hairs he refused to shave, but they'd turned gray, and it was hard to get a visual on them. I think I liked chest hair.

Luca looked at the helmet in my hands.

I hid it behind my back. "If you thought I was planning on riding this Vespa while buzzed, you're…"

"What?"

"It's against the law to lie to a police officer in Italy, correct?"

"Yes."

"Never mind then," I muttered. "Would anyone steal Nonna's Vespa if I left it here?"

"And you're going to walk home?" he asked.

"Looks like it."

Rosemary and Coronis made crude gestures behind Luca's back, and I very subtlety flapped my hand, hoping they'd stop. I didn't need him turning around to find them making kissy faces at each other. Why did everyone want to hook me up with Luca? I guess he had that ruggedly devastated look going for him. A sad widower always got the sympathy card, unlike a divorcée.

Luca rolled his manly eyes and his manly shoulders. "Put that on. I'll drive you back to Villa Venus."

"You?"

"Do you see anyone else not drunk around here?"

I looked at the merry square. Everyone was either giggling, leaning over tea lights, or kissing passionately. "Not really."

"Okay, then, let's go."

Luca straddled the Vespa like it was a wild horse he had to tame. He keyed the ignition, even going so far as to rev it slightly. When I didn't budge, he turned around to look at me, a question posed in the upturn of his eyebrow.

"You want me to hold onto you?"

"Unless you'd prefer to fall off."

"Fine, fine." I sat as far back on the tiny seat as I could, making sure there was room for Jesus, as one of my foster moms loved to say. Although the amount of times I caught her being rude to Jesus would have made Mary Magdalen blush, prostitute or not.

"What's wrong? Why aren't you putting on your helmet?"

"The latch is stuck."

Luca examined it and popped it open with his thumb. "Do you need me to snap it shut, too?" he asked dryly.

"I've got it, thank you."

Narrator: She did not have it.

Luca adjusted the straps, clicked the latch, placed my hands around his waist, and took off. The wind limited our ability to talk, but that was probably for the best. In my current state, I didn't trust myself to speak.

My body vibrated from the engine beneath it and from the hot Italian man between my legs. His abs were hard and ridged as I explored under the pretense of getting a tighter grip. Delicious.

Luca revved it again, and I let myself enjoy the warm bite of the trade winds off the ocean. It was easy to rest my cheek on his back and enjoy the smell of pine and cypress and Luca's own woodsy scent. I had a feeling he spent the majority of his day outside. He looked too big and primal to be kept indoors.

Luca motored to the villa and the Vespa puttered to a stop. I melted into him at the sudden stop in vibrations, my fingers clutching his stomach tighter. "Do you need help?" he asked, offering his hand.

He helped me down and removed the helmet, his fingers on the soft skin of my throat. As Luca turned around to clip the helmet to the handlebars, a little devil poofed up on my shoulder. She wore the clingiest red dress with a slit that went past her thigh.

I blinked slowly. "Are you real?"

"Did you say something?" Luca asked.

"Uh, thank you. Very kind," I rambled.

"You're welcome," he replied, walking the Vespa next to its partner and adjusting the kickstand.

"Go away," I panicked, flailing my hands at the little devil.

She sashayed around, parading her hips in silk. "I think you should go for it," she said, her voice tantalizing low and sultry. "You never know. Maybe you'll bang this out of your system. This is the new you, right?"

"First, I don't need to be 'banged' to love myself," I whispered.

"What's the second part?"

I crossed my arms. "I don't need to explain myself to you." Mostly because the second part was admitting there was no way I could fit into one of those slinky dresses anymore. Not gracefully at least. And getting out of it once we got back to his place? Mortifying. It would've been like a sausage casing. No one needed to see that. At least, no one who wanted to eat wants to see that. And I would not mind being eaten. Eventually. Once I was past the man maiming stage.

Devil-me flipped her hair over her shoulder and walked up to my ear. "I think you'll enjoy it." Then she disappeared in a puff of smoke. I shivered as Luca turned back around.

"I think you must have dropped this earlier." He handed me a tube of lipstick, his calloused hand brushing mine. "Do you have a key?" he asked oblivious to the inner war I'd waged with the personification of my slutty side.

"A key?" I repeated dumbly.

"To get inside." Luca raised that manly eyebrow, so like a hairy caterpillar, and I thought about stroking it.

"No! I mean, yes. Yes, I have a key." I patted my bag. "Thanks, again. See you around."

Luca's eyes gleamed. "So, you're planning on staying?" At my confused look, he said, "People talk. It's a small town."

"Everyone has been very welcoming." I fiddled with the tube of lipstick. "Yes, I think I want to stay."

He nodded slowly. "From one newcomer to another, be careful. I've found this town to be lovely, but also unpredictable." He moved closer, his eyes intense. Like he was remembering something. We held each other's gazes, and I felt little warm squiggles in my belly for the first time in a long time. Besides the quiet waves breaking below the cliff, our breathing was the loudest thing, and it easily fell into rhythm with each other.

"Thank you for taking me home, Luca." I closed my eyes and went on my tip toes—only to feel something hard grip my shoulders. I peeked under one eyelid. Luca held me at arm's length, his eyes sad. "Goodnight, Signora."

"Oh, I'm getting divorced," I said, my face as hot as my stomach had been seconds before, all the beautiful squiggles now writhing in embarrassment.

"My apologies. But even an unmarried, older woman would be addressed by Signora." He gave me a slight nod and lumbered off into the night.

If I thought that horrifying exchange was enough mortification for a day, that was before I woke up in the middle of the night, walking on the waves like Frankenstein's monster.

A glorious sound drifted on the wind, but somehow, it filled my head as if it were inside me, an ear-worm I couldn't escape. "Hello?" I asked, my voice sounding mangled and ugly compared to the melody.

It was black as tar outside with only a ghostly sliver of a moon shimmering on the ocean to light my way. My feet were wet. And my legs. I looked down. My entire body was half in the waves. Somehow, I had climbed out of my window, down the cliff, and tossed myself in the ocean.

"I must be dreaming."

The water licked higher, or I was sinking faster. "Okay, time to wake up," I told myself sternly. "Right now."

When the water reached my chest, I began to seriously

panic. This was not how I wanted to go. It wasn't as if I'd ever considered all the ways I wouldn't mind dying, but drowning at forty certainly wasn't it. I knew I should have called someone.

The singing began again and it was comforting. Maybe drowning wasn't the worst way. I heard it was peaceful. Once your lungs filled up, you sort of drifted off, unaware.

Oh yeah? My mind challenged my subconscious. *And how would dead people be able to tell us that?*

Good point.

Great. Now I was arguing with myself. Again. *Please, please, please, don't drown.*

A woman sat on a rock in the middle of the waves. Her mouth was open in a perfect O, and she was saying something.

"Help!" I called.

She smiled back and that's when I realized she wasn't saying something. She was singing. The siren. Nonna had called her Thessaly.

"Why are you doing this?" I sputtered, desperately pawing at the water. I had to get to that rock. Either I'd strangle the siren or knock her out. Both worked for me.

The singing paused.

Her talking voice was just as melodious, but it didn't have the forcefulness that made me want to drown myself. Now I was drowning because I was tired.

"What?" she asked. Her teeth were sharp and shone like saltwater pearls.

I made garbled, water-logged attempts to speak.

"What are you saying?" she asked. "I can't understand you when you're drowning and splashing around like that."

"Stop talking and help me then," I shouted, my lips barely above the water.

The beautiful woman with hair that matched the sea

closed her mouth. She looked at me like a confused barn owl, her head cocked to the side, before reaching out and tugging me the last few feet to her rock. She inched her toes away from where I was panting, half-drowned.

I took in lungfuls of deep, clean air, then celebrated not dying by sprawling on her rock. The siren simply watched.

Finally, I dragged myself to a sitting position and asked, "Why save me if you want to sing me to death?"

"You know… I don't know. In a thousand years, no one has ever asked me why."

"Okay, well I'm asking," I said bluntly. Now that I could finally lift my head and look at her, she truly was beautiful. Her eyes were Tyrrhenian purple and brilliant against her pale, blue-tinted skin. She had high cheekbones like royalty and soft pink lips. Silhouetted against the moonlit ocean, she looked like a fairy tale mermaid come to life, but swap the fins for razor-sharp teeth.

"I have to sing," she said. "Singing to me is like oxygen to you."

I wrung out my shirt and tried not to gag at the taste of saltwater coating my mouth. "I don't see the point in drowning people unless it's for fun or food. So, which is it? Are you planning to eat me?"

"I'm no cannibal," she said in disgust. The waves went higher, ripping me from my rock and tossing me around, again. "Why would you think that of me? You are nothing more than a puppet of men. You read their stories about me and believe it as fact."

"No! I don't know anything about this life. I promise. I just don't get why you want to randomly sing people to their death."

The waves receded. "I am cursed by the gods. This is my punishment. I am stuck on this rock and I haven't left in thousands of years."

I treaded water, choosing my words carefully. Instead of accusing her of anything, I said, "I could try to help."

Thessaly considered me for a moment. Her hair swirled blue and green, shimmering in the moonlight. "That wouldn't be terrible."

"I can research it tomorrow."

Thessaly nodded slowly. Then more vigorously. "Yes. Yes, I want to walk on the ground again. Can you do it?"

"I can try."

"Do it, and I will tell you a secret. A secret only I know."

"About what?"

"A secret about Aradia," she said firmly. "Now, go home."

Chapter Twelve

I WOKE up with Tiberius snuggled under my arm, snoring. Because of course I did. After a quick stretch routine that mostly focused on getting all of the cracks out of my ankles and hips, I went to percolate myself a cup of coffee. Or twenty. This was Italy. They didn't judge coffee consumption.

I stumbled out of my room, pulling out pieces of seaweed that were still stuck in my hair. That meant last night in the ocean with the siren had definitely been real. Thessaly wanted to be un-cursed. Should I tell Nonna? She'd saved me from the siren on my first day here, but I definitely didn't understand their relationship. It felt complicated.

When I got to the kitchen, Nonna was already there, humming and stirring something in a pot on the stove. It smelled meaty and delicious. The perfect hangover food, especially if there was gravy around and something to smother it over. Like biscuits. Oh, that sounded too good. Between night walking and drinking all that wine, it felt like I needed an exorcism, but I'd take some greasy food for now.

"Sit, Mamma. I'll have breakfast ready soon."

I took a seat and watched her add more crushed herbs into the pot as my mouth watered. I wondered if she made breakfast for her guests every morning. "Nonna, have you checked on Aurick yet?"

Nonna let go of the spoon, although the decadent smelling ragú kept swirling on its own. "Curses. I knew there was something I was forgetting. Can you watch this?"

"Sure."

"Do it lovingly."

"Um," I said, picking up the spoon and wondering what, exactly, stirring lovingly looked like. "Hey, Nonna. Do you think the reason you keep forgetting about Aurick is because he wants you to forget about him?"

Nonna stopped dead in her tracks. She put a finger to her nose and tapped it. "You know, you're pretty good at this *strega* stuff."

I basked in the moderate praise. The last time anyone told me I was good at anything was probably at the principal's office in high school after I'd beaten the snot out of some boy who grabbed my tit. I think the exact quote was, "Why are you so good at getting into trouble, Ms. Falcetti?"

I was always considered "troubled" by my teachers and foster parents. I considered them "troubled" too, though. Downright bastards, some of them.

Nonna headed to the back bedroom. There was a loud knock and some light conversation.

I stirred the ragú, lovingly, and considered last night, the siren, the dream that wasn't a dream, and my promise. I was so lost in my thoughts that I jumped when Nonna came back in the kitchen to announce that Aurick would be joining us for breakfast.

"Perfect," I said, rubbing my chest. At this rate, the old crone was going to give me heart palpitations.

A moment later, the back bedroom door creaked open, and the tallest man I'd ever seen shuffled out of his room looking dazed and confused. His clothes hung off him in large swaths, as if he had cobbled together pieces from a Big and Tall menswear outlet store.

I didn't fall for the pretty faces and scruffy beards. Italian accents—well that was harder not to swoon over, but I was made of stronger stuff now. I could resist Luca with effort. Aurick, on the other hand, I would have no trouble resisting.

"*Buongiorno*," he bowed. It was as awkward looking as him.

"*Buongiorno*. I'm Ava Falcetti. You're Aurick?"

"Correct." His voice was tinny and exact. Curt, almost.

Nonna shooed us to the table and served us both. There was homemade bread, butter, and grape jam. Carafes of orange juice, cold cuts, and croissants. A bowl of briny olives and feta that quickly became my favorite. It was a European feast.

"How long have you been here?" I asked, buttering a piece of ciabatta bread.

Aurick jerked his head up, shocked I was still there.

I waved my butter knife in a spiraling arc. "On Aradia. Not like planet Earth or something." Although I had to admit, I was curious about that, too. It looked like a long time.

"I've lost track of the days."

Nonna set down a plate of hardboiled eggs. "It's been at least a year, right?"

"Probably. Thank you, Nonna."

We sat uncomfortably silent for a few minutes, chewing. As Aurick swallowed his last bite, he stood, said goodbye, and went back to his room. I waited until the door shut, almost as quietly as him, before breathing.

"Oh, thank God."

"Odd, that one," Nonna agreed.

"What does he do all day?" I asked.

Nonna shrugged and popped an olive in her mouth. "You'd have to ask him."

"I get the feeling he wouldn't answer. Not directly, at least."

Tiberius finally rolled out of my bed, blinking blearily at the morning light. "*Buongiorno*, ladies." He picked up an egg and examined it. "Did I miss anything?"

"Only Aurick," I replied.

He froze, his eyes flickering to the back room. "Is that what that smell is?"

I started to ask what he meant, but stopped and watched in fascinated horror as he attempted to swallow the egg whole. Life was so weird.

"You should be careful," I began, but it was clearly too late. His eyes bulged and his tiny paws clawed at the lump in his throat. I jumped up and tentatively banged on his back, afraid I'd hurt him if I hit too hard. "Nonna!"

Instead of freaking out, she frowned. "How many mornings do we have to do this song and dance?" She made a complicated movement with her hands and muttered something under her breath, expelling the egg with magic.

I rubbed little circles on Tiberius's back while he gasped. "But they're so good," he finally said.

"I'll cut some up for you next time," I promised.

The espresso had already perked me up, so I decided to chance a few questions to see what Nonna thought of the siren. "What do you know about Thessaly? Has she always been here?"

"Why?" Nonna barked. "What did that old she-devil say about me?"

I held my hands up. "Nothing."

"You can't trust demons. Remember that, Mamma."

"She's a demon?"

"Of course. Sirens don't come from this world. Don't let her say any different."

"Okay, okay. I was just curious."

Nonna humphed and sniffed. She scooped up the dirty plates and dropped them in the sink.

"So, you two go way back?" I asked casually.

"You could say that."

Cryptic. I had a feeling I wouldn't get much help from her. Coronis and Rosemary might be more helpful. Surely everyone had to know about the sea demon living in their backyard.

Nonna dried her hands on an old kitchen towel. "What are your plans for the day? Did you want to go into town and see Luca?"

Now I was the one who jumped. "What?"

"Luca," she repeated. "He always takes his morning coffee at Rosemary's around now."

"Nonna, I literally just found my husband in bed with another woman. In no universe do I need to jump into some other man's bed right away." I didn't feel the need to tell her that merely thinking of Luca and his bed made my core heat up and my stomach do funny little flip flops. "Actually, I was hoping to find Coronis. Do you know where I could find her?"

"Also at Rosemary's." There was that sly glint again.

"I get the picture," I said, going to change and to

swallow a bottle of aspirin. That wrinkled crone was going to be the death of me yet.

"*BUONGIORNO!*" I called, walking into Rosemary's Bakery. It was warm in the golden morning light, and the smell of espresso made my head spin lightly, but I knew its reviving powers would soon be slipping through my system.

Rosemary came around the counter and kissed my cheeks. "Espresso, darling?"

"*Sì, per favore,*" I said, trying out my new tongue.

"Ah, look at you!" she laughed. "Anything else for breakfast?"

"No, Nonna fed me. But I would like to take you up on your offer to help in the mornings. If it's still on the table?"

"Of course. How about you start tomorrow? It will be fun, I promise."

"Okay," I nodded, looking forward to my career change. Anything would be better than selling insurance.

Rosemary jerked the machine to a stop and handed me the petite cup of foaming espresso. "Coronis should be in soon. Why don't you have her show you around today?"

"She doesn't have to do that. I'm sure she's got other things to do."

Yeah, I was digging a little. What did these people do all day? The island almost seemed locked in time. No commerce, no contact with the outside world, no internet. So how did Marla find it? Also, besides the food establishments and Luca's self-appointed *polizia* position, no one seemed to work. How did they all survive? The best I could figure, it was like some self-sufficient medieval village. Did people exchange vats of goat milk for Rosemary's espresso? And where did she get the beans? I had so many questions.

The bell over the door rang.

"*Buongiorno!*" Coronis sang.

"*Buongiorno!*"

"*Buongiorno!*"

I lowered my voice. "Now that we're all here, I wanted to ask you ladies about something. I had a little run-in last night."

"With Luca?"

I shook my head. "Thessaly."

At their confused faces, I clarified. "The siren."

Coronis almost fell out of her chair. "And you survived? What happened?"

"I talked to her. She's cursed, that's all. She claims she doesn't eat people and just wants to walk on the ground again."

"So she says," Rosemary scoffed.

I swallowed my next question as the bell rang over the door. Luca. He wore a light gray button-up shirt and slacks that made him appear professional, but laid back. It had been decades since I'd allowed myself to examine a male that way. Clearly, Jim had none of the same compunction.

Luca tipped his hat in silent greeting, and Rosemary got up from our table to serve him. He was an enigma, one I wasn't so sure I should decipher. It was too soon. I knew a reckoning was coming. For now, I was sweeping my emotions under the rug to enjoy my getaway. If Aradia was truly going to become my home, I'd need to process what happened. Would I need to see Jim and Marla ever again? God, I hoped not. But I should call the twins before they found out from someone else. That wouldn't be fun after all the times I'd laughed off their suspicions. Jim, a cheater? He was too lazy to record his own shows or make his own late-night snacks. How could he possibly find time to seduce my assistant? At any rate, I refused to involve the twins in their parents' problems.

"Darling, are you there?"

I snapped out of my reverie to see Rosemary and Coronis watching me sadly.

"There's no better place to heal than in the Italian sunshine," Coronis said, as if she had been reading my mind or, at very least, my emotions.

Rosemary agreed. "I was just telling Ava that you should show her around today."

"That's a lovely idea," Coronis said.

We finished our cups as Rosemary cleared the table. "Have fun, ladies! Tomorrow, it's to the grind for you, darling."

Rosemary winked and I realized the feeling in my chest was excitement. To find these women felt like a miracle in itself. Proof I could move on and find purpose in a new life. As we said goodbye and waved to Luca, I wondered how much he'd overheard. I guess it didn't matter. He was nothing more than eye candy at this point.

We walked into the warm, salty breeze. I let it ruffle the sun dress around my legs and marveled at how good it felt to do nothing more than enjoy the feeling of sun and wind on my bare skin. I let simple pleasures pass me by too often in my every day shuffle from work, school, and weekend sports clubs with the boys. Falling into bed only to zone out to television like every other couch zombie in America had taken its toll.

"Outside of the near-drowning with that siren, how have you been holding up?" Coronis asked. "For a MILF, you've taken Aradia in stride."

"I've always wanted to believe," I admitted. "It wasn't that far of a stretch, especially when I woke up to an astral projection of Nonna."

Coronis eyed me strangely. "Nonna did what?"

"Astral projected. That's what she called it, at least."

"Did she?" Coronis murmured. "*Stregas* don't typically have that power. Now, Nonna is much older than she claims, but I don't know if she's the oldest thing on this island. That would be Thessaly. Or maybe Marco."

"Is it rude to ask what Marco is? I keep hearing lion. Does that make him a lion shifter? Is that a thing?"

"It's a thing. This way." Coronis guided me down a quieter, cobblestone alley. "I have something special to show you. As for Marco, I think some of the residents might feel rubbed the wrong way if you were to ask, but I know you're genuinely curious. That's not a terrible trait to have. Marco is descended from the Nemean Lion. When he shifts into his lion form, his golden fur is impervious to weapons. He's practically indestructible. Marco and Rosemary have an epic love story I'm sure they'd love to gush about over wine some night. If you haven't noticed, they can't keep their paws and claws off each other."

"They do seem rather enamored, but maybe that's just my bitter jealousy talking. Up until a couple of days ago, I was certain my marriage was it. While not the most exciting or sexy marriage in the world, it was still the bed I'd made. What about you? Have you ever been married?"

"Oh, not me. I'd rather pluck my own feathers than settle down for eternity."

"Eternity?" I laughed. "Surely no one is immortal." Silence. I waited. More silence. Suspicion flared. "Coronis, is anyone here immortal?"

More silence.

"Wait, is *everyone* immortal?"

"Long-lived is probably a better way to put it," she replied.

"So, you're not going to tell me."

"Look, here's the church! The manuscripts in there can describe it better than I ever could."

I glanced up at the massive, red brick structure. It had a round apse in the back and a tall façade. Except for a few crumbling places near the ground, it was in remarkable shape.

"This is the Basilica of Aradia. It's an old Byzantine church from the sixth century."

I went silent as we entered the dark and quiet setting. It didn't appear that anyone still held services there, but the gold mosaics that covered the dome of the apse glittered in the candlelight.

Coronis pointed out a few. "Here are the stories of Aradia's founding," she whispered, surely feeling the power in the air the same as me.

I pointed to a beautiful woman sitting on a rock, surrounded by waves. "That looks like Thessaly."

"That is Thessaly, as you call her. We mostly refer to her simply as the siren. Legend has it that she was sent here as punishment by the gods. Then, the gods were banished during the Archon Wars thousands of years ago, and she was never able to appeal her sentence."

"The what war?"

"The Archon Wars were a series of great battles between the gods and supernatural creatures. The archons were our intermediaries to the gods. In most cases, direct contact with the gods meant dismemberment and death. The archons went between the realms with ease. Their name in ancient Greek means ruler, but we know them as Rulers of the Realms. During the war, they sided with the gods."

"What happened next?" I breathed, barely above a whisper.

"The archons were also banished."

"To where?"

Coronis lifted her shoulders and gave me an elegant shrug. "To another realm, I suppose. According to the Greeks, there were three. There is our realm here on Earth, the in-between is called Nibiru, and finally the realm of the gods is called Axis Mundi. Only demons, ghosts, and archons can pass through Nibiru. And only gods and archons visit the Axis Mundi."

"Wow."

"Life has been quiet in the thousand years since the wars. We supernaturals stick together. There are other islands like Aradia, but we are all shielded from most MILFs. Which is why Luca's and your presence is interesting."

My stomach dropped. "Is it?"

"Yes," Coronis said. "It means one of two things. Either the power around the island that keeps MILFs out is weakening…"

"Or?"

"Neither of you are human."

Chapter Thirteen

MY FINGERS TINGLED WITH ENERGY. Not human? I felt altogether too mortal. Thanks to my nighttime visit to the ocean, my muscles ached, including one knot in the middle of my back I couldn't even reach. And there weren't enough lotions and potions in the world to keep my crow's feet away.

I glanced guiltily at Coronis. I wondered if that was considered a slur in her world. I didn't mind the wrinkles. They weren't that deep yet, and they proved I used to laugh. I had had good times. My boys were a shining one, despite their naughty kid years and rebellious teen ones.

Clearly, I had been avoiding speaking to them. How exactly does one tell one's kids their father is a cheating jerk without destroying their relationship with said jerk? No matter how pissed I was at him or what he had done to me, they deserved to have us both.

I vowed to call them as soon as we finished touring the basilica.

"Over here," Coronis called, lifting up a dusty cloth

that covered the altar. "It's the names of the original priests."

We looked through the books for a bit, but they were rather boring. Finally, I got up the courage to ask about Thessaly.

"Is there anything here that would help us un-curse the siren? It seems unfair she has to be punished for eternity."

"She's a demon. Worse, she's a demon that got herself cursed by the gods."

I shifted my weight. "She was so wistful. I mean, what's the worst she could do?"

"You mean besides swim across the open waters sinking ocean liners at random?"

"Could she do that?" I asked, aghast.

"No idea. Most of the sirens I've met—which are like two and that was mostly by accident—aren't malicious and certainly not powerful enough to take down a whole cruise ship. It took a dozen sirens singing together to sink ships in ancient Greece and those were triremes."

"You lead a crazy life."

Coronis grinned. "You have no idea." She turned to look at the golden mosaic of the siren. "Oh why not? She's never been murderous to me. In fact, I haven't heard one instance of her luring someone from the island to their death. She just stays in the water away from prying eyes. At most, we hear mournful songs at night."

"So you'll help?"

"Yes," she confirmed. "I'll get Rosemary to help, too."

"There is one thing," I said. I knew if I was going to ask for their help, I should be completely honest. It was how I would want to be treated.

"What?"

Deep breath. "Thessaly mentioned a secret. Something

only she knows. She promised to spill once I un-cursed her."

Coronis raised an eyebrow. "Now that is interesting."

"Do you think she really has a secret?"

"No way to know until we do it. Oh, how exciting. While Rosemary had a point and we do enjoy the quieter life, a little innocent adventure never hurt anyone."

"Is it still innocent if it includes freeing a demon?"

"Good point, but we haven't had a real problem to solve in way too long. Then you show up, and suddenly, we've got flickering ghosts and secret-wielding sirens!"

"I aim to please." In all honesty, Aradia was going to have to pry my cold, dead fingers from her island before I left. From the mundane to the extraordinary, this was the most purpose and fun I'd had in a long time.

Coronis led me to a part of the church that felt older than the rest. "The manuscripts of our founding are over there."

Suddenly, the church rumbled, and I had to grab onto a stone column until the tremors stopped. Wide-eyed, I looked at Coronis. "Do you get earthquakes often?"

"Earthquakes?"

"Yes, didn't you feel it?"

Coronis looked at me with concern in her eyes. "Ava, are you quite alright?"

The shaking started again, more violently this time. Cold sweat broke out across my palms. It was happening again. Like I'd taunted Aradia into action.

Coronis reached out to help, but the earth threw me to the ground. My arm caught on the sharp edge of a wooden pew, and a gash opened from my elbow to my wrist. I screamed, and Coronis rushed over to cradle me. "Shh, let me look at it," she said, gently lifting my arm to the candlelight. "Has anything like that ever happened to you before?"

"Once in St. Louis on the morning I found Jim and Marla together. The same day I found Aradia and decided to leave."

"Did it feel the same as this one?"

"Exactly the same," I replied fervently. "What if neither of them was actually an earthquake?"

Coronis made a sound suspiciously like a caw, her head bobbing up and down. "You're right. That was no earthquake. It was Aradia reacting strongly to you for some reason."

I didn't like the sound of that, but then Coronis closed her eyes and covered my arm with hers. Immediately, a warm, watery sensation flooded my senses.

"Coronis?" I interrupted, unsure of what was happening.

"Give me a moment, darling. All magic comes at a price."

"You're a healer?"

"You don't know much about mythology, do you?" At the slightly hurt look on my face, Coronis burst into laughter and patted my hand. "Don't worry about it. MILF schools are notoriously bad about teaching our true history. Crow shifters like me are descended from the original protector of the Greek princess, Coronis. Apollo, god of light and music and a bunch of other shit, fell in love with the princess, but she was unfaithful during her pregnancy."

"Sounds juicy."

"It gets better. A white crow, dispatched to spy on her, told Apollo. In his godly wrath, he killed the princess and her lover and scorched the crow black. When he felt remorse, he saved the baby by cutting him out of Coronis's womb and named him Asclepius—the god of healing. Crow shifters were gifted in healing matters during the Archon Wars as an incentive to side with the gods."

"Wow. So your parents named you after the princess, even though she wasn't a crow?"

Coronis blinked. "Something like that." She took her hands off my wound. "There. Better?"

"That's amazing!" I turned my arm back and forth. The blood had crusted over, and where there once was a huge gash, I could only find a thin, watery line. "Wait, so Princess Coronis had an encounter with the gods. It sounds like the archons weren't always needed."

"Even in a benign encounter, the princess still ended up dead," Coronis spat. "Tell me where the glory of the gods is in that?"

I noticed her ice white hair beginning to rise as if touched by static electricity, but then Coronis smoothed it down. "I'm sorry. The gods tend to get me worked up. Their cruelty knew no bounds. Our world is much better without them."

"So, the crow shifters didn't side with the gods even after their gift?"

"No," she said shortly.

"And the archons are bad or good? I'm having a hard time keeping up."

"Neither bad nor good, but they did side with the gods. I'm of the mind that we're better off than we've been for centuries. The gods would have held humanity back, keeping them as their slaves. Not that humans aren't their own worst enemies, but at least they're beginning to learn."

"I won't lie. I feel like my head is spinning. Between the shaking earth and a whole new world…"

Coronis put her arm around me and helped me to my feet. "It's a lot to take in. I'm also of the mind that you're not a MILF. Aradia is much too careful about who she lets into the veil. This is a haven."

"So how did Luca get in?"

"That was the year everything was askew. Right place at the right time. Maybe the island sensed he needed healing. Maybe it sensed you needed it, too."

"Then why does it keep trying to hurt me? Honestly, it's all wonky now, too. It could very well be another case of the veil failing," I said, feeling a teensy bit disappointed.

I was already preparing myself to accept that I was nothing more than Ava Falcetti, human being. Maybe it was the sudden blood loss. Maybe it was the magic that had now worked its way through my veins. More than likely, it was finally looking at the loss of my former life— the only one I'd known for twenty years. Whatever it was, it brought hot tears to prick at my eyes.

"I think I need a minute," I told Coronis and weaved my way through the pews to the sunshine-filled doorway.

Once outside, I took a few deep breaths, resting against the doorframe. Coronis came up behind me and gently led me to the steps. "You don't want to hang around in liminal spaces. They're extremely weak parts of our world."

"Liminal spaces?"

"Yes. Gateways. Door frames. The in between places. The ancient Greeks used to think that was where demons hid, waiting for their victims, so they skipped over them. They were right. Demons do. Remember what I said about Nibiru? It is the ultimate liminal space where all demons are born. Your Thessaly was banished here to our realm for her punishment."

Feelings of being completely in over my head threatened to engulf me. I sat woozily on the steps and rubbed my eyes with the heels of my hands. "I don't know if I'm cut out for this. What if I just went back home? Would all of this knowledge leave? Would I go back to being a clueless MILF?"

Coronis gave me a sad look. "I'm honestly not sure. Is that what you want?"

I looked around the beautiful, travertine marble of the buildings, the black cobblestone streets, the relaxing fountains. I pictured Rosemary and Marco. I remembered our apertivo hour and how Rosemary had offered me a job.

And, yes, I pictured Luca. Who wouldn't? For the first time in years, I felt like I was finally waking up. Life could be so much more than ironing underwear and sitting in a cubicle. I'd needed a kick in the pants to get here, but now it was done and I'd arrived. How could I let anybody—or anything—take that away from me?

"No, but I need to contact my sons. Let them know I'm here and what happened. Do you know how I can get a signal?"

"We have one working landline that we use to order supplies. We're always trying to get Luca to add lipstick to the list, but he insists on 'essential' supplies only. Which to him are food and toilet paper."

I jumped to my feet. "Wow, you just answered seventy-five percent of my questions. Well, maybe forty-five percent. I don't know. I have a lot of questions."

"You talk a lot, too."

"It's the hustler in me. And I definitely need him to add women's underwear to that essentials list. I've had to wash the ones on my ass every day. So," I rubbed my palms together. "Where's this phone?"

"Luca's. I thought that was obvious."

I sat back down. Of freaking course.

Chapter Fourteen

LUCA'S APARTMENT was like his style of communication. Sparse.

He opened the door wearing a suspicious expression and a pair of low-slung athletic pants. He was bare foot and bare chested and clearly waking up from an afternoon nap.

Despite the nap, he looked exhausted. He had sunken, shallow cheeks and dark bruises under his eyes. Did he have a secret girlfriend no one knew about keeping him awake at night? I resisted the urge to peek around his shoulders, but it hardly mattered. The one-room apartment was empty except for brown boxes stacked against the walls and a twin bed with a thin, cotton sheet.

"Ciao!" Coronis said happily, explaining in rapid-fire Italian that we'd like to use his phone. She'd told me on the walk over that his place used to be the old storage room for supplies, but when he came, they just shoved a bed in the corner and let him stay. He'd been so sad and out of it that he was more than thankful for a place. In exchange for room and board, he took care of their little spats and complaints. No major crimes ever happened, and he wasn't technically connected to the mainland's *polizia*.

Luca opened the door wider, but I had the distinct feeling he didn't want to let us come inside. His scowl deepened and he blocked half the doorway with his body so we had to scoot around him. Maybe someone should tell him about liminal spaces. Not me. After our failed kiss, I did my best not to make eye contact.

Coronis secured the line and I gave her the boys' number. Once it started ringing, she led Luca to the table in the far corner so I could have some privacy.

While I was positive they wouldn't pick up a strange international number, I planned to leave a voicemail with a time I'd call back tomorrow. It rang five times until it went to their recorder. My heart swelled at the sound of their voices, and I had to turn around to make sure Luca didn't see a tear slip down my cheek.

"You've reached Josh and Jacob Longsworth. If you're calling about class notes, we didn't take them. If you're a chick, leave your name, number, and place of meeting."

Okay, I'd kill them.

"Leave a message!"

I sucked in a breath. "Hi boys, it's Mom. I love you both so much. I'm in Italy, but don't worry. I'll call you tomorrow at five p.m. your time. That will be fine, right? I don't want you to miss the dorm dinner time. Shoot, maybe six? No, no, let's stick with five, and if you can't make it, I'll just leave another message and come up with a better time." My voice began to crack. "I love you both," I repeated. "Study hard. Don't worry about me. Italy is wonderful. I can't wait to see you in a few months. Bye, I love—"

The recording cut me off because I was a rambling lunatic. I hung the phone in the cradle and sniffed up the snot already working its way down my nose. I couldn't believe how amazing it was to hear their voices, even on a recording. Even talking about women as "chicks."

Oh God, crying twice in one day had to be some sort of record. I couldn't remember the last time I'd been so emotional. Jim called me "checked-out", but I merely kept my emotions close to my heart where they were better protected. Once the kids started elementary school, life became hectic. We found ourselves snapping at each other for little things and not saying sorry. Or the apologies were couched in defensive excuses until it didn't feel safe or even worth it to air our grievances. Instead of divorcing, it was easier to get up, make breakfast, send the kids to school, go to work, eat dinner, watch television, go to bed. Rinse, repeat.

I guess now that we didn't have the fear of messing up the boys with an ugly divorce, Jim decided it was time to pull the ripcord. The bastard didn't have the grace to do it without Marla in my bed, and for that, I doubted I'd ever forgive him. Give me twenty years and a hot Italian lover. Then I'd consider it.

Chapter Fifteen

I WOKE up in the ocean again, but this time, I was more prepared. Which is to say only a mouthful of sea water went down my lungs before I remembered to hold my breath.

"Are you trying to kill me?" I asked peevishly as I dragged my body up Thessaly's rock. "I have my first day of a new job tomorrow. Now I'm going to have puffy eyes, and I'll probably burn all the bread and spill the coffee. Rosemary is going to wonder why she hired me, and I'll have to quit to save us both the embarrassment, but it'll still be awkward and she'll never talk to me again."

Thessaly sat with her arms crossed over her bared chest. For however many thousands of years old she was, they were still perky as hell. "You said you would un-curse me."

"I said I would try, and I am trying. I went to look at old manuscripts in the basilica today, but Aradia stopped me."

"Aradia knows what you are."

My fingers went cold as I watched the sea demon toy with her blue-green hair. "Do you know what I am?"

"Of course. I think others know as well."

"Who?"

What if my new friends were lying to me? Wouldn't that just take the cake? Then I might have to let Thessaly drown me, since I'd been so desperate for friendship that I believed any old thing out of their mouths. I was pathetic. I—

"What are you doing?"

Thessaly's voice snapped me out of my fog. Waves swirled around me, keeping their distance, as I stood on the sea bottom. Little fish flip flopped around me, gasping at the sudden night air. With that moment of clarity, the water gushed back in, and I was drowning. The water was cold and dark. It was a sucking vortex taking me away. Thessaly dove under the waves and held me to her cold body as she swam to the rock.

"What was that?" I asked as she let me go. My teeth were starting to chatter, and I rubbed my arms up and down.

"You have a gift."

"Are you sure? That didn't feel like a gift."

"No." She eyed me wearily. "Perhaps it's a curse."

"Tell me what you know!" I grabbed at Thessaly, but she backed away, snarling. Suddenly, her teeth sharpened to fangs and I sank back. "Please tell me. Do you know what it's like to suddenly wake up after so many years dragging through life? I'm finally awake and I'm desperate to know the real world around me."

"No," Thessaly said flatly. "Cursed sirens don't sleep."

"I'm sorry," I said, because it felt like the right thing to say in the moment.

"You could help me sleep. If you un-cursed me."

I knew I wouldn't get anything else out of her with that look on her face, although at least her teeth were back to normal. "Okay, okay. I already promised, but I'll re-promise if that helps. I'll figure out how to un-curse you."

She glared at me.

"I promise."

"Good."

"Will you give me a hint now about who I am? Am I like… the chosen one?"

Thessaly laughed so hard, I thought she might fall off her rock. I wasn't as amused.

"No."

"Fine, give me a hint then."

"I just did. You're not the chosen one."

I frowned. She was enjoying this. "Give me another. Consider it an act of good faith. Or an upfront payment. Half upon signing, half upon delivery."

She leaned in close enough to see her purple eyes glowing in the dark. "I'm certain. Yours is a curse. Pure and simple. I know a godly curse when I sense one."

I shuddered involuntarily. "Will I die?"

"That depends on many things. Not from the curse, though."

"Like…" I waited for her to fill in the blanks.

"Find my cure and I will help you."

"*Quid pro quo*, eh? You sure you're not human?"

Thessaly sneered.

I sat on the rock, still shivering, and peered through the moonlit ocean at Villa Venus sitting on the far-off cliffs of Aradia, which I'd have to scale in my nightie. "So, this is weird," I began, looking sideways at the siren, "but could you sing me back to my bed?"

Thessaly narrowed her eyes in confusion. "Why?"

"I really don't enjoy the idea of having to breaststroke.

I'd rather be hypnotized or knocked out or unconscious or whatever supernatural stuff you deal in."

Thessaly's face barely changed, but when she opened her mouth, a beautiful, haunting aria swept me off to dreamland.

"Are you getting enough sleep?" Nonna asked as we rode into town. She had joined me as a show of support for my first day of work. It was sweet, but I think Tiberius talked her into it so they could get free biscotti.

I jumped, mostly because I'd been dozing on Nonna's back for the mile trundle into town. "Hm? Yes. Just getting used to sleeping alone."

That was true. Despite our marriage being full of silence, Jim and I had still slept in the same bed every night. It was probably why I'd wanted to escape the moment I found Marla in it. Learning to sleep alone was oddly disconcerting. It didn't help that Thessaly's words would not stop weaving through my mind, making sleep all but an impossibility.

I could think of plenty of times where I'd felt cursed, but that was mostly when I hit all the red lights on my carpool days. Or, you know, when I found my assistant tangled up in my bedsheets. Or was that a blessing?

The same questions swirled and haunted me until Nonna killed the engine, and I realized we were there. At the ungodly hour of 4:45 a.m.

"Rosemary will have your head spinning so fast, you won't even realize it's afternoon."

"Great."

Apparently, I was going to have to learn to be a morning person.

Rosemary handed me a white apron, no frills. "We serve only specialties since we're a small bakery. Basically, we took a survey to find the top ten things everyone wanted in the mornings and these are it. Changes to the menu are subject to a new survey and a town meeting."

"You're kidding, right?"

"Harpies rarely kid."

I tied the apron around my waist and washed my hands as Rosemary explained the elected pastries.

"Bomboloni donuts are fried to order, but we'll make the yeasted dough now and keep it in the fridge. Torta della Nonna, no relation, is a custard cake with pine nuts. I make that the night before so it sets up by morning. We also have cornettos, which are like croissants, but we fill ours with Chantilly cream and pistachios. Then there's chocolate hazelnut biscotti, lemon ricotta cannoli, tiramisu, sfogliatella, seasonal fruit tarts, bread and marmalade, and of course, a pizza for my Marco. We change the toppings depending on what's available. This week, it's speck and eggs, because Marco hates sweets."

"Except for you, *cara mia*," a loud voice boomed.

"Was that Marco?" I asked.

"Of course. He's next door in his taverna preparing the wood fired oven. That's where we'll bake the pies and pizzas."

"But how did he hear?"

Rosemary shrugged. "Lions have very good ears."

I made a mental note to be very careful about what I said as Rosemary showed me how to whip the cream for the bomboloni and cornettos. Apparently, that was about as far as she was willing to let me go on my first day.

"Next, I'll teach you how to do pastry cream."

"Maybe tomorrow I'll do the dough!"

Rosemary gave me a smile. "I like your enthusiasm. Not a chance, but I still like it."

After two hours of straight up hard work, I stood back and took in the glorious view of Rosemary's refrigerated glass showcase at the front of the bakery. There were golden pastries, pillowy creams, and bright pops of red raspberries and strawberries with flecks of emerald green pistachios. It was a thing of beauty. Besides my twins, I couldn't think of anything I'd ever been prouder of in my entire life.

As soon as it hit seven a.m., the bakery flooded with customers. Rosemary had a line out the door and around the square. Everyone chatted as I gamely tried to remember the difference between latte macchiato and caffè macchiato. One was milk with a drop of coffee and one was coffee with a drop of milk, but I kept mixing it up.

After the rush, Rosemary ordered me to take a break, and I slumped in a chair next to Nonna.

"You're doing great, Mamma," she promised.

"Am I? I feel like a chicken running around with my head chopped off."

"You are."

"Which one? Doing great or a headless chicken?"

"Both. Hey, why don't you invite your boys here?" Nonna gestured for more espresso. "Let them see your new life!"

"Here?"

"*Certo che sì!*"

"I miss them fiercely, but I couldn't possibly ask them to miss classes."

"Oh, what's a weekend here or there?" Nonna said, waving away my concerns.

"Lots of money. Jet lag for the entire trip. I could go on."

"Pah," she said.

I took a sip of my third espresso. "You know, our American Thanksgiving is coming up. I could see if they want to come for the week." I didn't mention how wonderful it would be or how it would instantly make me the cool parent. No contest. I'd stuff one warm, fluffy, oozing bomboloni in their faces, and they'd be putty in my hands. Jim who? Finally, after years of being the strict one, which was just so stereotypical, I could be the fun one. They were no longer my baby birds to parent into functioning human beings. They were adults. And I would woo them with sugar.

My face must have had a dreamy look because Tiberius waved his paws in front of my face. I jumped.

"Now that you're awake, can I have this?"

I scowled as he took the last piece of my bomboloni and stuffed it in his mouth without waiting for my response. Nonna scooped him up and tucked him in her pocket. "We'll see you back at the villa?"

"Yes. See you for dinner."

They shuffled out as the late morning crowd began shuffling in, each looking for a little caffeine and sugar to start their day. But I also noticed a few repeat customers for their second pick-me-up. I was barely one to judge, though, as I finished my third. Tonight, I definitely needed some sleep, which meant I had to find some information to give to Thessaly. She was as relentless as her waves.

As the crowd died down, Coronis sauntered in to grab the last of the cornettos. She looked fabulous as usual, wearing a pencil skirt, high heels, and a polka dot blouse that tied at her left hip. Rosemary joined us, and we told her the gist of what happened at the basilica. Then, I filled them in on Thessaly.

Coronis almost choked on my Chantilly cream. "Again? That demon is too bold."

"She just wants to get out of the water," I insisted. "Although, I'd prefer if her summonings weren't while I was sleeping."

Rosemary, however, was quiet. "She said you were cursed?"

"Any ideas?"

Coronis tapped her nose, which, when I thought about it, did look a little beak-like. "And Aradia wouldn't let you see the manuscripts."

"Yeah, that was weird. I'd like to do some research, but I don't think you have the internet or a library, right?"

"Not in this realm," Coronis said.

Once again, I had no idea what that meant. "Any chance you know much about de-cursing a siren?"

"Never heard of it happening before."

Suddenly, the bell jingled as someone attempted to push open the door ten minutes after closing. Our heads snapped up like marionettes on a wire. A tall man with light blonde hair, piercing blue eyes, and a strong jawline stood at the entrance to the bakery. He looked vaguely familiar. There was something captivating about him, and I wasn't the only one who felt it.

Rosemary stuttered something about "Welcome to Bakery", forgetting her own name and possessives for a moment as she unlocked the door.

Without taking her eyes off the newcomer, Coronis wiped some flour from my elbow and a smear of chocolate off my chin. She was a good friend like that.

"*Ciao*." The man inclined his head and then turned to look at the case of baked goods—what was left of them anyway.

"I'll take that one." He pointed to the last cannoli.

"And perhaps a latte macchiato if you still have the machines running."

That voice. There was something very familiar about it.

"Yes, yes, of course." Rosemary ran off to do his bidding while I stared without remorse. He looked like he'd stepped off the pages of a GQ magazine for classy, older men. He wore a long, black coat with a short, upturned collar and simple jeans with a black shirt underneath.

The man must have felt my stare burning into the back of his skull. He turned around with a slight smile at the corner of his mouth. "*Buongiorno*, Ava. I hope you like your new job?"

I jerked so hard, I fell into Coronis's lap. She yelped and helped me back up.

After we were sufficiently red in the face, I gave him a once-over. "I'm sorry. This sounds horrible, but do I know you?"

"Ah," he said softly.

"Did we meet at apertivo hour? Because I wasn't really myself that night—"

"No," he said, his smile turning into a smirk, clearly enjoying my discomfort. "I haven't been into town yet."

My heart thudded in my fingertips. "No way... Aurick?"

His face was smooth and shiny with a marmoreal gleam. Not even Botox achieved that kind of results, and he could still make facial expressions without appearing constipated.

He bowed slightly at the waist before turning to thank Rosemary and accept his macchiato. With one swallow, he downed the hot liquid and handed it back. "*Grazie mille*. I'll try not to be late tomorrow, Signora." He turned to me. "Ava, shall I see you at dinner at tonight?"

I opened my mouth, but nothing came out. Was this gorgeous man asking me on a date?

"At Nonna's," he clarified.

"Ah, yes," I said, a bit disappointed.

He gave us one last brilliant smile before turning to go. Rosemary locked the door behind him and staggered back to her seat, fanning herself. "Don't tell Marco," she whispered.

"What? That you acted like a nerdy school girl who'd just been approached by the high school quarterback for her homework?" I teased.

"*Che?*"

"Never mind," I said quickly. "That was not the Aurick I met yesterday. He looks like he had a face lift at some expensive, celebrity spa in the South of France. Or a face transplant."

"Does he?"

"Yes. Yesterday he could barely keep his eyes open or string three words together. Now he's a certified hunk. What type of supernatural creature does that make him?"

"Vampire," mused Coronis. "The older they are, the more sleep they need."

"But Nonna said he eats garlic."

"Ah, that wouldn't matter too much. It's more the dismembering of their head that harms them."

"Or…" Rosemary trailed off.

"Or what?"

"Maybe a mummy. But they're quite rare."

"He's pretty pale for an Egyptian mummy," I pointed out.

"There are other types of mummies. Not just in history, like the Incan mummies, but individuals who have been turned into one. Actually, ancient mummies are the rarest. Most have crumbled into dust by now. I've heard of a few on the Council, but they spend most of their days in their wrappings."

"It felt like you said council with a capital letter."

When Coronis laughed, it sounded like a bird chittering. It was cute. "Yes, darling. The Council of Beings was formed after the Archon Wars to govern supernatural creatures. We couldn't go around letting blood mages, vampires, and demons prey on innocent MILFs. The Council polices supernatural beings. Keeps them in line. Investigates complaints. That sort of thing."

"They used to," Rosemary snorted. "When's the last time you've heard of the Council doing anything other than sitting in their hall and gorging on gossip? We don't really need them anymore."

"Things have been quiet everywhere for a long time," Coronis admitted. "It's like I told you before, supernaturals keep to their islands of refuge. Aradia tends to be a Graeco-Roman haven. Someday, you should visit some of the communities near the Scottish Isles. Selkies know how to throw a party."

I rubbed my temples in tight circles. "Once again, my brain feels like it's going to burst."

"What are you going to do this afternoon?" Rosemary asked. "We could show you around and teach you more about the supernaturals."

"That sounds amazing, but I'll probably go home and take a nap. You know, to prepare for Thessaly. She has no sense of personal space, but then again, she is a siren."

"Would you like us to be there tonight?" Coronis asked.

I cocked my head at them, thinking. "Maybe. It would prove I'm trying. At very least, you might be able to get more information out of her."

We walked outside into the brilliant sunshine and ran

straight into Luca, who was pretty much a brick wall in motion.

"Luca, I didn't see you today for coffee. Is everything okay?" Rosemary asked.

Luca looked at us guiltily. "*Scusi*, Signora. I overslept, but don't worry. I ate something at home." He looked over his shoulder. "Who was that?"

"Aurick," I said. "He's the other guest at Nonna's villa."

Luca's eyes narrowed, but it was so slight I almost missed it. "Interesting. Please let him know I am available if he needs anything."

"I will tonight, when I see him for dinner."

"He asked you to dinner?"

"Oh, no," I said at the same time Coronis and Rosemary said "Yes!" which just confused everyone. "Dinner at Nonna's," I clarified.

"Ah." Luca looked thoughtfully at me, and I was sure my fluttering pulse was visible to every supernatural on Aradia. Damn their heightened senses!

He turned to go. "I'm going to meditate near the cliffs today if anyone needs assistance."

"Assistance in paradise, Luca?" Coronis laughed.

"You never know. Good day, ladies." He shuffled off toward the ocean.

"Poor man." Rosemary shook her head. "He's clearly in so much pain. I couldn't imagine losing my Marco." She gave me a sly eye. "What Luca needs is a good woman to help him move on."

"Yeah, heard that one before. But my shop is closed until I clean out the cobwebs and figure out me."

"Didn't he seem interested in the fact that Aurick was having dinner with our dear Ava tonight?" Rosemary asked.

"As a matter of fact he did," Coronis agreed.

I rolled my eyes at both of them, as a cold wind gusted through the square. It rustled the ivy growing around an old Roman aqueduct and swept through our hair. I shivered. "Did you guys feel that?"

We stood still.

"A ghost wind."

"Where's it coming from?"

The wind grew stronger and we struggled to stay upright as we looked for the source. There, flickering to life under the stone arches, was a Roman Centurion and his faithful mastiff. The ghost still wore his breastplate with etchings of myths, and the dog had a permanent string of slobber hanging from its jowls. The Centurion stumbled, dazed and confused. He reached out his arms covered in rotting leather greaves and looked at us in shock, as if he couldn't believe he wasn't still dead.

Rosemary and Coronis called out to him in Latin, which I understood even less than Italian. The Centurion began gesticulating while the mastiff let out a series of plaintive barks. Whatever was happening to the ghosts of Aradia, they didn't like it.

"What is he saying?" I asked, as the ghost began to flicker, just like Piero. Every time he appeared again, his mouth went wider and his eyes more frightened.

"He's confused—discombobulated. He doesn't know how he got here or even how he died for that matter. He keeps wanting to go back to his camp and his commanding officer."

"What should we do?" I asked. "Lead him to the cemetery?"

"Nonna will know how to help," Rosemary said. "She's the resident *strega*."

Before we could corral the Centurion, however, he

disappeared. We tentatively spread out in a circle, calling out in Latin, but we didn't find so much as a drop of drool.

Coronis caught my arm. Her eyes were wide. "Darling, don't say anything in front of Aurick. We don't really know him—or what he wants."

"You think he has something to do with this?"

"All I'm saying is that it's odd. Suddenly he's awake and all these ghosts appear."

"I have a better question," Rosemary said. "Why are they all so scared?"

Chapter Sixteen

WHEN I WENT to Italy to find myself Elizabeth Gilbert style, I didn't think I'd actually find myself staying at a *strega*'s villa, sharing accommodations with a mouthwatering man who was quite possibly a vampire, and waiting on my two new supernatural friends so we could interrogate a siren at midnight in the middle of the ocean.

Yet here I was.

When I got back, Aurick was in his room and Nonna was rolling sun-dried tomato ravioli. She set me to work, harvesting the rest of the bug-eaten lettuce and kale from her dilapidated garden. I cut out the buggy parts, salvaging what I could because, apparently, we didn't waste around here.

"How was your first day, Mamma?"

Chop, slice. "Pretty great. A lot to take in, but great."

"I told you. Everyone falls for Italy eventually. Now that you've settled in a bit, I wanted to show you what else I found at the cemetery."

I paused, feeling myself perk up at her words. "Really?"

Nonna plopped the fresh ravioli into a boiling pot of salted water. Fresh Pomodoro sauce bubbled away on the back burner. "Yes. Go into that drawer." She pointed at the bottom one near the hearth. "Pull out the tube, open it, and bring me the scroll."

I did as ordered, finding a brittle roll of parchment. It had red and black ink scrollwork and long, looping cursive letters. The moment my fingers touched it, whispers drifted up, and I almost dropped the scroll.

"Careful, Mamma!"

"Aye, sorry. But I think I heard it say something!"

"That's just its protections."

"Why does it need protections?"

Nonna rinsed the lettuce and dried them in a tea towel before dousing them in lemon juice, olive oil, and fresh chunks of parmigiana cheese from her wedge. "Most witches have grimoires, right?"

I shrugged. "I guess."

"I have Septimius Severus's magic scrolls."

At the pregnant pause, we both stared at each other, the scrolls dripping curls of smoke onto the floor. "Is that a Harry Potter thing?" I finally asked.

If looks could maim, I'd be without a finger.

"Don't be silly. Severus, the Roman emperor. He buried secret scrolls of magic in the tomb of Alexander the Great. Alexander's tomb used to be a pilgrimage place before it was lost sometime in the fourth century during the riots and earthquakes in Alexandria. The scrolls were secreted away, meaning I had to obtain them much later."

"How do you lose a tomb?"

"You'd be surprised," Nonna said darkly.

By now, Tiberius had smelled the food and wandered into the kitchen. I wondered where he went when he wasn't mooching food off of Nonna. Or what good a familiar served besides witty banter.

"I'm giving them to you to look over. For some reason, I haven't been able to open them in decades, but you're making me rethink all kinds of things. Maybe I can't read them because they're not mine anymore."

"Wow, that's generous. But like Tiberius said, I'm not a witch, so I'm not sure why I would be able to access them."

Tiberius jumped on my shoulder and sniffed my hair. "What I said was that I wasn't sure if you were a witch, and I stand by that."

"Being unsure?"

Tiberius nipped at my ear.

"Careful! I don't have a rabies shot," I protested.

Nonna shooed him away. "You never know, Mamma. Something tells me they're yours now."

I shrugged. It wasn't the strangest thing to happen to me in the past forty-eight hours. Then I headed to my room to change and tuck the scrolls into my luggage.

Although I knew I wanted to stay forever—and that was before attractive men started popping up all over town—I hadn't unpacked. It seemed too presumptuous.

Everything was happening at breakneck speed, and tonight would be another challenge. Just because Jim jumped into bed already with someone else didn't mean I needed to, even if we hadn't been together in, well, months. Or was it years?

I sat on the homespun quilt and looked into the gilt mirror hanging over the dresser, trying to decide what to wear. If the little devil wanted to poof up and give me another pep talk, that would be great.

I waited. Nothing happened. Maybe I had to be drunk.

Finally, I got up and chose a simple pair of jeans and

nice shirt. Nothing too fancy, but the jeans did show off my curves. I threw my dark hair into a half-ponytail and gave my lashes a few swipes of mascara. I had work to do tonight anyway. I bent closer and did a quick inspection of my face. Those damn chin hairs were back, and my eyebrows were even bushier, if that was possible.

"I thought they were supposed to be thinning with age," I muttered, going to grab my tweezers.

My hair, too, felt fuller. More luxurious. I resisted a peek down below. There must be something to this Mediterranean diet. It had barely been a week and my hair and nails were noticeably longer—stronger even.

Aurick was already seated when I came back out. I hated to admit it, but he certainly filled out a chair with his large frame. He wore a pair of black jeans and a black t-shirt with a Scandinavian light jacket in moss green. His blonde hair was slicked back, and for some reason, it sent shivers down my belly. He'd taken time to dress with care.

He got to his feet to pull out my chair, and I suddenly found myself wishing I could run back and swipe on some blush or lipstick.

"Ava, you look wonderful." He kissed the back of my hand, like some courtly gesture, and scooted me under the table. "Here, I opened a bottle of Chianti."

I accepted the stem, apparently mute now. Aurick gave me a long, lingering smile that actually made my face warm to the touch. He was smooth.

It's his magic, I reminded myself, although I had absolutely no idea if that was true.

Whatever it was, Nonna broke the spell immediately by yelling at us to pour her a glass and try not to spill on her tablecloth. Aurick laughed. "I wouldn't dream of ruining such fine material," he said, motioning with his hand at the tattered, worn out tablecloth before us.

We served ourselves helpings of hand-rolled ravioli and salad. Then I pulled out a few pieces of tiramisu that Rosemary had given me.

Nonna sat back, smoking a pipe. Large rings of smoke drifted lazily to the ceiling as we digested our meal.

"Have you gotten a hold of your twins yet?" she asked.

"Not yet. I told them I'd call again tomorrow."

Aurick went to pour me another glass, but I waved him off. I'd need a clear head for Thessaly. "You have children?" he asked.

"Yes," I said, glowing slightly at the thought of them. I hoped they weren't out partying all night. "They're hardly children anymore, though, sad as that is to admit. My boys are seventeen. They graduated a year early and went to college a few weeks ago."

"Good for them," Aurick said kindly. "Education is not to be squandered."

"Thank you."

Nonna's eyes twitched. "Seventeen, you say?"

"Yes."

"Good, strong boys. Almost men."

Weird comment, but Nonna was a nutter. That, I knew. Nice, sweet, great cook, but a nutter.

"Almost. They'll always be my baby boys, though." I'd always remember fondly the worm phase, the t-ball and ice cream phase, and their warm snuggles. Quickly, too quickly, it moved to the braces phase and girls phase and the "Can we have a phone, Mom?" phase. Jim always found ways to wiggle out of saying no directly to all their demands. I didn't mind saying no. It was our jobs. What I minded was not being the one they went to when they needed a yes.

Nonna's clock chimed ten. I promised to meet the ladies at half past, so I stood up to do the dishes. Aurick's chair scraped after mine. Suddenly, he was towering over me, his hands in the soapy sink. "Ava, please, I can take care of this."

Don't swoon! You're too mature for that.

"I, uh, thanks," I stuttered, unsure what to say when a man offered to do the dishes. "I better be getting to bed. Rosemary really has me working hard lately. I think she enjoys being a boss. Well, good night, Aurick."

Nonna pulled me aside as I attempted to make my escape. "You're sneaking out," she said matter of factly.

I didn't try to deny it. The truth was written all over my face.

"What's this about now?"

I sighed. "Thessaly."

At Nonna's hiss of dismay, I held up my hands. "She doesn't deserve to be chained to that rock. We're trying to figure out how to un-curse her."

Nonna eyed me fiercely. Tiberius, sensing he was summoned, jumped on her shoulder for a quiet pow-wow. "You feel it in your gut?" she finally asked. She made a fist and smacked it into her stomach twice. "You feel it right here?"

I nodded. "I do."

"Good enough for me. I'll distract Aurick for the rest of the evening."

"Although that's really no hardship," Tiberius said, and I officially had to scrub from my brain the idea that even a chipmunk found Aurick attractive.

"Thanks, guys."

I went to my room, waited twenty minutes, and slipped out of my window like a teenager, thrilled at the escape. It made me feel young again. I used to break into houses at night when I was in between foster homes to steal food from their pantries. It felt safer than gas stations or grocery stores where cops sat waiting like fat spiders in the corner to take you to juvie. But a home? If—big if—an adult caught me, they'd see a scared teenage girl, small for her age with large eyes, holding a wad of bread and cheese. Some would slip me a few dollars, others ran me out. All of them called some type of authority, but by the time the cops or social workers got there, I was always long gone.

I'd lost most of that edge once I'd met Jim. He hadn't swept me off my feet, but he'd saved me from the life of a high school dropout, working full-time as a cocktail waitress. Love hadn't been much of a factor. Not when you're desperate.

He'd offered stability, a home, a job. I took it, no questions asked. It was probably why I was so resentful after a few years. I hadn't worked my way out of a hell-hole situation. I'd taken his charity, giving him children in exchange for a roof and food. It was one of the reasons I loved the bakery so much, because I was learning a trade. Even if I had to flee at some point, I could find work as a baker.

The moonlight drew a path across the ocean through a grove of cypress trees and up to the villa. I could follow it all the way to Thessaly if I wanted. I began to wander away from the yard, deeper into the grove. An eerie caw echoed across the cliffs.

"Coronis?" I called softly. "Rosemary?"

Two huge winged creatures leapt from the nearby trees and landed next to me in the shadows. I recognized Coronis in her crow form immediately. Her glittering black eyes came up to my waist. Rosemary took a bit of getting used to.

"Don't scream, darling. It's just me."

I swallowed my gasp, although my heart was still

beating fast. From the neck up, she was Rosemary. Sweet, frizzy-haired, pink-cheeked Rosemary. From the neck down… she was a bird.

"Good God, why are you both like that?"

Coronis cawed once while Rosemary looked guiltily at the ocean. She still had her human head and could speak, but only said, "It's easier."

Finally, it dawned on me. "Are you scared of Thessaly?"

"She *is* a siren."

"And you *are* a harpy."

"Harpies are nowhere near as terrifying as sirens," she protested. "Sirens lure men to their deaths. Harpies annoy you and steal your food."

"You don't annoy me," I told her seriously.

"That was back in the old days."

"Okay, well I'll meet you over there. I've got to swim. It's that rock jutting out under the path of the moon."

"Darling, I can carry you. We also used to kidnap people for the Furies."

"Oh."

Rosemary spread her wings and jumped into the air. "Don't worry. I've never kidnapped anyone against their will."

Coronis cawed and Rosemary shot her a look. "That doesn't count."

Rosemary's claws slipped down the back of my neck, and she lifted me by my shirt. Seconds later, we were airborne. I let out a squeak at the sudden ascension as she glided down the cliffs, my toes skimming the waters. In no time, we were on the rock, waiting.

"Thessaly?" I called into the waves. "Are you here?"

A movement disrupted the moon path, like a shark in

the water. Rosemary's claws dug deeper into my biceps, and I winced. "Rosey, dear, you're hurting me."

The tension eased slightly. "Sorry. I thought it was the siren."

"It probably was. But it will be fine. I promise." I cupped my hands around my mouth. "Thessaly?" I called. "It's Ava. I brought Rosemary and Coronis to see if they could help with our problem."

The waters around the rock began to ripple. An eerie, haunting music that sounded somewhat muted bubbled up from the deep. The current got stronger, and the two birds took to the sky while I climbed to the top of the rock.

"Thessaly? We're here to help! So you don't have to drag me out of bed this time."

Suddenly, a water spout erupted and the beautiful siren shot out of it like the Little Mermaid. She threw her head back, her blue-green hair flinging water droplets on the three of us.

I did a slow clap. *Clap, clap, clap.*

Thessaly came down with the spout, cocking her head to the side. "Why are you clapping so slowly?" she asked, her melodious voice floating on the currents.

"It's a sarcastic clap. You know what? Never mind."

Thessaly put a finger under her chin. She paused, looking me up and down. "I see it's happening."

"What's happening?"

"The curse. Nice hair, by the way."

Everyone stared at my hair. I patted it awkwardly.

Coronis and Rosemary transformed back into women and stood on either side of me, their hands linked. Thessaly watched from the water, amused. Her chiton was silky white floating at the surface.

"Is Ava not a MILF?" Coronis asked, glancing once at me.

"She is not," Thessaly confirmed.

"What is she?"

Thessaly smiled, one baring all teeth. "That truth she will find in the basilica. If Aradia lets her. Now have I proven myself? Have you come to rid me of this hideous curse?"

Guilt flowed through me. "We're trying. Honestly. But it's hard to find anything useful."

Thessaly shuddered at the words, and water swelled around the rock. "I just gave you something useful. Trigger your powers and un-curse me if that's what it takes!"

"Trigger what now?"

"Go to the basilica. Stop asking me," Thessaly said.

I moved higher, but my foot slipped on the soft algae and I began to fall. Coronis and Rosemary both dove to catch me, but Thessaly sprayed a plume of water and gently righted me.

With a silent glare into each of our faces, she announced, "Help me, and I will save you from the evil stalking the island."

Then she was gone.

"Well, she's a confusing one," Coronis announced.

Rosemary nodded. "Demons."

I shivered in the sudden cold and shock of being wet at night. No matter how many times I yelled her name, Thessaly never returned.

As Rosemary flew me back over the cliffs, I thought about the implications of Thessaly's words. Evil on Aradia. Powers. Magic. Odd things had always happened around me, but did that really mean I had powers?

"Do you believe her?" Coronis asked.

"I don't know," Rosemary admitted. "She was lying about one thing."

"What?"

"I don't see how she could possibly save us if she's no longer here."

We let that marinate as we said goodbye and trudged home. Well, I trudged through the cypress trees. They flew, those lucky birds.

Chapter Seventeen

IT'D BEEN another week and we were no closer to uncursing Thessaly. Worse, every time I tried to enter the basilica, Aradia forcefully threw me on my ass.

Coronis and Rosemary took turns going in to read the ancient manuscripts and transcribe them from memory, but it was tedious and slow since there seemed to be a barrier to taking anything out as well. As a result, we were no closer to figuring out the basilica's secrets and if it held the truth to who I was.

Hopefully it wasn't something embarrassing, like a cockroach shifter. If that was a thing. Although, I'd bet cockroach shifters didn't die easily.

"I had no idea this island held so many mysteries," Rosemary lamented into her espresso martini.

"Me neither," said Coronis. "I can't decide if I'm elated or terrified."

"Let's go with elated," I suggested. "Otherwise I'll feel bad for coming here and starting an existential crisis. It's bad enough when I'm having one of my own, but to give the existential bug to everyone around me just seems rude." I swirled a glass of red wine and popped a bacon wrapped date filled with parmigiana cheese into my mouth.

I loved this life. Except for the basilica that seemed to have it out for me. But honestly, I'd put up with more to get less in life before. This was downright delightful. I adored mysteries.

"Darling, we're glad to have you," Rosemary covered my hand with hers and squeezed. "And a little existential crisis now and then never hurt anybody."

"I doubt that, but thank you. Wow, these dates are so fresh! They taste like pure honey and then the salty cheese and bacon..." I gave her a chef's kiss and ate another one.

A shadow covered our table. We looked up to see Luca. He always dressed so professionally. A button-down shirt, carefully manicured hair and fingernails—important, since they'd be touching you—and not too tight pants. It was as if he really expected to be running down a criminal or petty thief, but still wanted to look professional.

"Can I have a minute?" he asked. "With you, Ava," he added when we all stared.

"Of course. Be right back, ladies." I left my wine and walked a little ways to the fountain. Luca took a Euro and flicked it into the water with his thumb. He handed another one to me. "Make a wish."

My mind churned at this new side of the suddenly mysterious *polizia*. "Okay," I said slowly, taking it from his fingers. His touch was warm and sent shivers down my belly. Even he seemed taken aback by the sparks. When I glanced up from our hands, his face had an unfamiliar look. Almost hungry. For me.

He cleared his throat. "How was your dinner with Aurick?"

I lifted a shoulder. "Well Nonna was there, so... fine?"

"Fine. Hm. And are you planning on staying for a while longer?"

"Looks like it. I love the quiet life here and all of the culture and history steeped in every stone and tree. I do miss my boys, though. They started college, so I'd be without them at home, too, but it's still an adjustment."

"If you'd like to use the phone, please don't hesitate."

"Thank you." I made a little wish, gave the coin a kiss, and threw it in the fountain. We started walking around the square and into the quiet alleyways. "Do you have children?"

Luca shook his head. "It was never in the stars for my wife and me."

The silence stretched out between us, which wasn't really my style. I took a deep breath and went for the plunge. "May I ask how your wife passed?"

Luca's eyes were pain-filled. He was still very much in love with her, and I would have no hope of competing with that. He laced his hands behind his back and stared into the distance for a moment.

"She died for me," he said shortly.

"I'm sorry," I said softly, not pressing any further. I could take the hint.

We continued to wander. Finally, he got up the courage to tell me why he had asked me to join him. "Would you like to get dinner with me tomorrow?"

I stumbled over a cobblestone, and Luca caught me before I fell.

"Excuse me?"

"Where two people eat food and get to know each other better."

"Right, a date. It's been a while, but I still understand the concept."

"If it makes you feel better, it's been a while for me, too."

I stopped walking to turn and face him. Post-affair Ava wasn't going to play the dancing-dating game. I was going to be blunt. "I have to admit I'm curious. I heard you haven't dated since the passing of your wife. Why now? Why me?" When he gave me a shocked look, I added, "Like you said, it's a small town and the gossip is fierce in Aradia. As the two newcomers, so to speak, we get the most attention."

Luca faced me, too. We were near the ancient Roman ruins of free-standing columns and aqueducts. I couldn't help but think he would have made a fine warrior, just like that Centurion, but that kind of thinking wouldn't help unless I understood his motives.

"Honestly?" he asked.

"No. Dishonestly."

Luca started, then gave me a wry smile. "Funny. The thing is, I'm not sure you'll like the answer."

My heart twisted a little, but I stood a little straighter. Whatever this man had to say wouldn't affect me. He had no place in my life—how could it wound me?

"You remind me of my wife." He said it quietly, fervently.

Well that was unexpected. "Me?"

Luca nodded. "You even look similar. I assume you have Mediterranean heritage by your olive skin and dark hair?"

"My twins gifted me one of those DNA ancestry tests for Christmas one year," I admitted. "I never knew my parents, and they thought it might help, but the genetics people were flabbergasted. It came back one hundred percent Italian. I guess not even native Italians are one hundred percent."

I could have sworn I saw his eyes glow at that, but then I noticed what was actually lighting up his entire face. The Roman Centurion ghost and his faithful mastiff had reappeared. Crap! Had I summoned them with my thoughts?

I had to get Luca away. There was no way I was going to be the one to ruin the town's ten-year streak of keeping Luca ignorant of the supernatural.

"Wait, do you see that? Something is glowing," Luca said, resisting my efforts to investigate a fascinating looking cracked cobblestone behind him.

"Nope, just the moon," I lied with fake cheerfulness.

"It looks almost human-like."

I scoffed. "*Et tu*, Luca? Come on. There's no ghost here."

"There's something here."

"Maybe it's indigestion. Did you have the spicy Calabrian crab pasta at the taverna tonight?"

"Yes..."

I clapped my hands. "Well, there you go!"

"To be clear," Luca said, "What you're telling me is that bad seafood is making me hallucinate?"

I shrugged. "I'm just spit-balling. It could have been the peppers."

It wasn't a very convincing theory, but I was desperate. Fortunately, the ghost chose that moment to fade out, perhaps sensing it wasn't a good time. When Luca turned back, he was gone.

"We should head back," I said, relief flooding my body.

Luca reluctantly agreed.

I took his hand and forced him to look at me and only me. No ghosts, no distractions. "One more question."

"Okay."

"Why now?"

"*Anche in paradiso non è bello essere soli,*" he said in his sonorous accent. "Even in paradise it is not good to be alone. Besides, you're very... fascinating. Shall I pick you up tomorrow night? If it's too bizarre because of what I told you, I'll understand."

"It's fine," I said. Then more forcefully. "Yes, that sounds great, but I can meet you at Marco's. It's no bother."

"No, I'll pick you up. It's only proper."

As we walked back to the taverna, I couldn't help but wonder if it was that Old-World quality that made Luca want to pick me up or if it was something else. Rather, someone else. A certain, mysteriously charming man living under the same tiled roof.

Chapter Eighteen

AS SOON AS I got back from Rosemary's Bakery the next morning, I dove into Nonna's grimoire, which were really Septimius Severus's scrolls. I didn't know how to feel about that. I never realized how much I'd relied on the internet until I didn't have it. I hadn't learned about the Roman emperors before I dropped out of school to work. Thinking about my lost education inevitably made me think of Jim. He was always so embarrassed when someone asked where I went to college, and he loved to constantly remind me that without him, I wouldn't have had a chance. No diploma, no degree, gaps in my work history from raising the children. What was it about me that pissed him off so much?

"Perhaps I may be of some assistance," a disembodied voice announced somewhere near my left ear.

I flung my hand around as if I was swatting a fly. "Piero! You have to stop sneaking into my room like that."

My Renaissance Romancer shimmered to life like a mirage. "I'm sorry, Signora. I close my eyes when you…"

His eyes tracked down to my lady parts, and he waggled his eyebrows.

"Piero! I'm going to kill you again!"

"There's no shame in pleasure, milady," he said, floating just out of reach. "We knew that best of all in Tuscany. Shall I find a lute to serenade you the next time you pleasure yourself?"

I launched a lace doily at his head, but it passed through without the desired effect. He held up his hands, and the feather in his cap jostled as he bowed. "No? Then let me help with your study of the scrolls. I studied them extensively in the glorious Medici court."

"These scrolls?"

"Of course. Everything of power eventually made its way to our court."

Despite my anger at his intrusion, I had to admit I needed the help. Nonna was constantly napping, and Tiberius couldn't shake the need to stock up for the winter, including storing walnuts in my suitcase. Even though he was only inhabiting a chipmunk's body, the rodent instincts were strong.

I put down the hairbrush I was planning to eviscerate him with. "Why did you study Severus's scrolls?"

"Severus merely found the ancient scrolls. The Book of Thoth was famous for centuries before and after in certain esoteric circles. Even Isaac Newton, that hack, may he rot forever and ever amen, tried to unravel the mysteries inside."

I moved past the Newton hatred and into the mysteries portion. "What was the mystery?"

"Immortality, of course. The Book of Thoth contains writings from the god himself. Its real name is the Emerald Tablet."

My hands froze over the brittle papyrus. "It's not emerald. Or even pea green. It's also not a tablet."

"Not to you. I saw it change once under the hands of the master mage John Dee in the court of Elizabeth I. While I never want to witness that particular trick again, I can help you with the more mundane passages." He rubbed his translucent hands together and drifted over the text. "Oh, yes. I forgot about that bit."

"What?" I peered over the lines.

Piero shuddered. "I guess it's fine now, but last time I incanted these lines…"

I gave him an encouraging continue gesture.

"I sort of exploded myself."

I practically pulled a muscle in my calf jumping away from the papyri. "These scrolls caused your death?"

"Yes, but reading the text is different. As long as you don't incant, it should be fine."

"Should?"

"Let's see, shall we?" Piero traced the Latin with a fingertip. "*Verum sine mendacio, certum, et verissimum. Quod est inferius, est sicut quod est superius.*"

"What does that mean?" I whispered, glancing at the door. I hoped Aurick couldn't hear Piero. Something told me that he'd be more than interested in what was happening in here.

"'Tis true without lying, certain and most true. That which is below is like that which is above."

Something sparked in my mind. I blinked a few times as images wavered to the surface. A woman. The scrolls. A dark passageway under stone arches. "Piero?" I asked, uncertainty marking my voice. "Did you accidentally—"

With a pneumatic pulse, I felt my body bounce and I was there.

. . .

Looking over my shoulder, I continued, my heart pounding in my fingertips and adrenaline coursing down my legs in a cold spurt. It smelled like rotting leaves and decaying earth in the cavern, and the small space was as black as tar.

My stolen body threw a small orb of blue light, illuminating the corbelled walls. This felt familiar. The place, the movement. Without having to blindly grope, I knew where to shine the orb. There it was. A small door glowed under my ghostly light. It was short; I would have to bend to get through it. I brushed away the undergrowth around the handle, found an ancient ring of bronze, and opened it with a creak. The passageway ended abruptly, and I could see a diamond of white at the far end. Vertical lines of text, hymns, and protection spells were carved into the stonework. I squeezed the orb into my fist, extinguishing the light. He was there. Fear, knowing what was ahead, mingled with something else. My ambition. It was all-consuming and vengeful.

On tiptoes, I crept along the dank walls, seeping moisture so far beneath the surface of the earth. The diamond grew as the tunnel rose. It smelled cleaner. Like lemons and pomegranate. I inhaled, enjoying his scent. I had given him the sleeping potion myself, but he was strong. There was only a little time before he fought against the magic.

Quickly, I vaulted over the secret wall and allowed myself a quick glance at the four-poster bed. Silk drapes billowed in the breeze from the open window. His eyes were closed, but his lids fluttered as if he were in a deep REM cycle. I knew better. He was no human and he did not dream. He was fighting me.

The scroll was tucked under his arm. Delicately, I wiggled the papyri back and forth until I freed it, unleashing a hunger I'd never experienced before. I knew I would rather die of thirst than let go of these words.

He may have found me, but I would know his most intimate secrets.

He may have dragged me home, but I would rise again.

The scroll dripped gray-white vapor and hummed slightly. My

fingers trembled as I unrolled it, the ink barely dry on the glyphs. Ravenously, I scoured the scroll's secrets. His life's work. A story fit for the gods. I was so absorbed in it, I didn't hear the first creak. Or the second.

In an instant, the god's hands were around my throat. The crush of his power was more terrifying than being hunted, and cold fear rolled down my body. He struggled through the fog of my sleep spell, but he was still stronger than me.

"What are you doing in here?" His voice was quiet, but full of menace. Our reluctant truce forged over the last few weeks, broken.

I fought to control the shivers and look him in the eyes. "If I am to be brought back bound—" he snarled at that, tightening his grip on my neck, but I persisted. "Yes, Thoth. Bound like a savage beast. If you insist on dragging me in chains, then I will know."

"Even for you, Runaway Goddess, it is too much."

"Nothing is too much for me."

The pressure released and I staggered back, massaging my throat and wheezing. Why had he let me go?

He laughed once. Then again.

Soon, he was laughing so hard that an eerie feeling of wrongness took seed and began to sprout. Somehow, he had outwitted me, and it pleased him.

I screamed and the moon shattered.

IN ANOTHER WHOOSH, I was back in my bed, shaking off the silvery remnants of the vision. The problem was, it felt more like a memory, something in the distant past. Worse, I didn't know whose memories I'd hijacked. I hadn't seen the face of the Runaway Goddess, but it was odd that the memories appeared after touching Nonna's grimoire. Nonna, who claimed to be 115, but clearly wasn't. Nonna, who claimed to be a simple *strega*, but could astral project. Things weren't adding up.

Piero looked at me with concern. "Signora," he began, but fell silent. He staggered a moment, then his eyes bulged. He looked like he was in great pain.

"What's happening?" I sat up, alarmed at the grotesque look on Piero's face. "Was it the spell?"

The ghost moaned and grabbed at his throat, contorting in unearthly shapes. "Help!" he gasped.

Chapter Nineteen

I SHOT out of my room, shaking and desperate to find help. Yet, as soon as my hand touched Nonna's bedroom door, I froze. She was the one who gave me these scrolls, and she clearly had her secrets. Then there was Aurick. For all I knew, he was the one killing ghosts, or sucking them dry, or worse. What did I know about the supernatural world?

Seriously, was Tiberius, a talking chipmunk, really my best option? That seemed absurd, especially since I only trusted him because he was cute and furry. The real Tiberius, the one inhabiting the body of a chipmunk, could be anything.

I dropped my hand and tiptoed away, but it was too late. A door creaked to my right. It was Aurick.

He stumbled out of his room, looking sleepy. "Is there a fire?"

I hesitated. "Nothing. No fire. Just… excitement." I nodded vigorously. "Yeah, I found a new path today, and I thought Nonna might like to join me on a little walk."

Aurick watched me carefully. I always felt like he was

playing chess while I was stuck on checkers. And it only took a glance. "I'll go with you. Despite my, ah, lengthened stay on Aradia, I haven't seen much of it beyond the villa."

I swallowed. "Maybe some other time." I looked at my wrist. "I forgot. I've got an appointment. In town. Soon. Ish."

Aurick raised an eyebrow. "You're not wearing a watch."

"Internal," I tapped my wrist again. "It's a gift."

"What time is it right now?"

"Four forty-two in the afternoon."

Aurick looked at his watch. "Ah-ha! Wrong."

"Well what time is it?"

"Four forty-three. Actually that was pretty good. Right. Well please let me know when you'd like to take that walk, Ava."

"I will." We said our goodbyes and I scooted back to my room.

"Piero?" I whispered. "Come back."

Suddenly, as if I actually had summoned him, my Renaissance Romancer reappeared, rubbing his chest and heaving as if he'd run a mortal marathon.

"Piero! What happened?"

"Milady, I don't understand. Something was sucking at my essence, pulling and yanking. It felt hungry. Vengeful." He stared at the scrolls. "I knew I shouldn't have read them again. Their power is too dangerous."

"You think it was the scrolls?"

"Impossible to tell. We have barely scratched the surface of their secrets."

I stuffed the scrolls in my suitcase and zipped it up. Fortunately, I really did have an appointment in town to join the ladies for our wine hour. We'd been extending it from Thursdays and Fridays to pretty much every night of the week, but only a glass. Some of us had honest work to do in the mornings. Rosemary had even mentioned letting me proof the yeast soon. Then again, she was a few centuries old, so her soon and my soon may be decades apart.

"I'll ask the ladies what they know when I see them, okay? You stay away from the scrolls."

Piero didn't need to be told twice. He had already put several feet between himself and the text and was busy making the sign of the cross.

I jumped on the Vespa and went straight to the taverna. I wanted to tell them about Piero and the Runaway Goddess. Being supernatural themselves, they could have some good insights—or even know her. But Marco was alone, wiping down the glasses with a rag when I entered.

"Ciao," I greeted him breathlessly. "Is Rosemary around?"

"Ciao, Ava," Marco's eyes hardened a little. "She's actually at the basilica."

I studied him. Cats didn't hide their emotions well, and this one was silently hissing. "What's going on, Marco?"

He took a deep breath. "Ava, I appreciate that you've come and upended your life to begin anew, but you're upending my Rosemary's, too. You're running her ragged between researching at that creepy basilica, teaching you how to bake, and staying up all night gossiping like Nonna."

I bristled. "I'm not forcing Rosemary to do anything she doesn't want to do."

"I'm not saying that."

"Then what are you saying?"

Marco flamed red under his voluminous beard. "She's too tired at night."

I stared at him until, finally, it dawned on me. "Oh my God, Marco. If she's too tired to have sex, tell her to teach me the secrets of yeast and I'll open the bakery a few days a week. That way you two can sleep in. Together."

Marco, more sheep than lion, turned around and pretended to put away a stack of clean glasses. "Thank you," he muttered.

Part of me found it sweet that he was still so in love with his wife after all these years, but bring it up to her. Not me.

"Actually," Marco said, drying his hands on a towel, "now that I think about it, she's been gone longer than she should. Do you mind watching the taverna while I check on her?"

"Of course."

"Thanks. I'll be right back." He untied his apron. "I'm not usually this worried."

"I understand, Marco."

"It's just, with the ghosts and all, we're on edge, and I don't know what I'd do without her."

"I get it, Marco. Now, go check on Rosemary."

He threw me the keys. "Just in case." Then he was gone.

I wandered around the old bar imagining what the place would've been like in 1260. Was everything shiny and new? To me, it felt like this place had sprung up like Athena from Zeus, fully formed with a patina already in place. Was it possible that Marco had opened it? I couldn't imagine having the same job long enough to get a pension, let alone hundreds and hundreds of years. No job was that much fun.

The door swung open and I jumped. "Sorry, unless you can point to the beer or bottle of wine you'd like, I'm afraid—oh! Luca, I didn't recognize you for a second."

He shifted his weight uneasily, and I had a feeling he didn't like to be caught off-guard. "Is Marco here? I wanted to grab something to eat before I went on my rounds."

"You go on rounds?" I asked.

"How else would the *polizia* keep a presence?"

I got a better look as he approached. The man looked exhausted. "If you wanted to take a nap, I'm sure someone would be happy to do your rounds for you," I said. Maybe I should take a page out of the Runaway Goddess's book and drug the poor guy so he could get some decent sleep. Lost goats and broken fence disputes could wait a day.

"I'm fine," Luca said. "Marco?"

"He's not here, but he'll be back soon."

"Marco's gone?"

"But he'll be back soon."

Luca couldn't help but crack a grin. "Ah, okay. I think I have some leftover bread and cheese, so I'll manage not to starve."

I considered the kitchen behind me, finally gesturing to it. "I could probably make you something. I'm sure Marco wouldn't mind if I touched his stove. Right? How does a grilled cheese sandwich sound?"

"You'd be surprised," Luca said seriously. "That's Marco's second love. The gesture is thoughtful, but I'll manage. I will see you tonight still?"

"Yes," I said quickly, having completely forgotten I'd agreed to a date. So much had happened in only a few hours, and yesterday already felt like a lifetime ago.

At that, Luca thanked me and left, which was a good thing. Five minutes later, two figures burst in, chattering excitedly. I jumped to my feet. "Rosemary? Marco? What's going on? Did you find something?"

"Ava!" Rosemary kissed me on both cheeks and lugged me out the door. "Lock up, I have something to show you."

All three of us stood at the stone entrance to the basilica, the closest Aradia let me get. "Marco, walk through again," Rosemary said. "Show Ava."

Marco exhaled loudly, but did as he was told. He entered the church and weaved between the pews, rubbing his chin on everything. "Happy? Would you like me to do a little dance? Light a candle and say a prayer? Desecrate a tomb? What are we going for here?"

Rosemary's eyes were shining. "See?"

I stared harder at Marco, who was now rubbing his butt up and down a stone column like a stripper pole. "Um… you might have to help me a little here."

"Marco," she called. "Go down to the crypt."

My eyes widened as Marco pulled open the trap door and sank out of sight.

"Now do you see what I mean?" she asked.

"He can get through," I whispered.

"He can get through," she agreed.

A croaky voice rang out across the cobblestones. "Mamma! What are you doing? I've been looking everywhere for you."

It was Nonna, hobbling at the speed of a rabbit. Although I was beginning to wonder about her—she was clearly hiding something from me—I was still glad to see her. "Nonna, something strange happened with Piero, that Renaissance ghost. I'm not sure, but I think someone was trying to kill him. For real this time. Do you have any idea what that could mean?"

"No, Mamma, I don't. Perhaps we should visit our

friends at the cemetery. See what they can dig up with those old bones."

"Oh, that's a good idea, but I can't tonight. I have a date."

"A date?"

"With Luca."

Nonna grimaced, and I felt a flare of annoyance. "Aren't you happy? You were the one pushing for this!"

"Eh," she shrugged, as Rosemary laughed.

"Are you serious?" I asked, but Nonna chose that moment to go selectively deaf.

Marco came back to the door. "I'm sorry, love, but I don't understand what you think you've found."

"You're descended from the Nemean Lion."

"I'm aware."

"Your fur is impenetrable."

"Once again, I know."

Rosemary gave his beard a loving stroke. "I'm really going to miss it."

Marco backed away, alarm lighting up his face. "Oh no. No, you don't. I love you, *cara mia*, heart of my heart, but no."

"Marco." Her voice was low and sultry. I shifted my weight uncomfortably as she nuzzled his ear, nipping it slightly. "I promise to do that one thing," she whispered.

Marco's head snapped up. His eyes searched hers. "The thing we talked about?"

She nodded.

"You promise?"

Rosemary winked and Marco began to purr. "Fine, woman! Shave me, take my fur, but you can never take my manhood."

Nonna slapped him on the back. "That's the spirit, you big pussy cat! Now what's this all about?"

Chapter Twenty

THE LION ROARED LOUDER, and Rosemary wrung her hands together. "I'm so sorry. Did I nick you again? Maybe someone else should do this. My hands are shaking."

Marco clearly wanted to shift back, but he stayed as a lion, waiting patiently. Whatever Rosemary had promised must've been worth it. I had to admit, I was curious. What went on in other couples' sex lives? Mine had grown so staid the last few years, I wasn't sure what to expect if I started dating again. Luca's square jaw came to mind. He hadn't dated in over ten years, either. We could go slow together.

I felt my face heating up and did my best to shake the images out of my mind. *Focus*. Piero's afterlife depended on this.

I grabbed Rosemary's hands and squeezed them. "You've got this. Take a drink of water and steady your mind. Deep breath in. Deep breath out. Good!"

"You're right. I can do this." She took hold of Marco's mane and began slicing precise rows.

While we waited, I filled Nonna in about the basilica

and how Thessaly thought I could trigger my powers inside. Nonna grumbled a bit at the siren's name, but she finally admitted, "That old demon might be on to something. Best go find out."

I nodded, the images from the tunnel ringing in my mind. I couldn't escape them. Since I'd seen them after touching Nonna's grimoire, I decided to take a chance. "Nonna, have you ever heard of someone called the Runaway Goddess?"

The old woman lurched and I caught her hard.

"You have," I said. "I see it in your eyes."

Nonna rubbed her elbow. "*Sì*. But where did you hear of her?"

"I didn't hear. I saw it in the scrolls."

Nonna's eyes darted to the left at Rosemary and Marco, who was growling low in his throat.

"Nonna," I pressed.

"Yes, yes," she fluttered her hands. "The Runaway Goddess, the Distant Goddess, the Wandering Goddess. They are all her names among others. But she is gone, just like the rest of the gods."

"In the Archon Wars?"

"No, before that. Much before that. She is a primordial being who read the tablets and was punished. She is nothing to worry about. Focus on your task at hand—figuring out who you are."

Interesting. Marco let out a roar, but this time, Rosemary only admonished him instead of getting flustered.

"I didn't even draw blood that time. Stop making me nervous!"

Marco settled back down with his huge head on his paws, but his tail kept twitching. Soon, he'd be completely hairless, and I wondered what the man Marco would look like without all his golden hair. Would the lion look more like a house cat?

Twenty minutes later, I had my answer. A very bald, very hairless, very large man. I could tell Rosemary was trying not to laugh, but Marco wasn't buying it. He kept muttering in Latin under his breath.

"And a pox on your family," Nonna said indignantly.

"Yes, no need to curse everyone, my love." Rosemary ran her hands over his bald head. "It's a little pointy at the top, but I like it."

"Just remember your promise," Marco growled.

Rosemary ran her finger down his chest and handed me the pelt. I had to admit, it was weird. And still warm. "Do you want to go to the basilica right now?" she asked.

I checked the clock on the wall. It was already five, and I was supposed to meet Luca at eight, but I didn't want to wait. "Sure, but let's hurry." I turned to Nonna. "Can you check on the ghosts in the cemetery? Something is spooking the ghosts here, and I want to know if they're affected."

She nodded. "We'll meet back at Villa Venus. Don't fret. We'll get to the bottom of it, Mamma. Now go."

As I turned to leave, Nonna gripped me by the shoulders and held me for a moment. "Listen, Mamma. I know it's scary. But girls develop before boys for a reason. We are the true leaders, nursing our men from day one. We gave them comfort and healing and tempered their rages. We are designed to lead. Matriarchies outnumbered patriarchies in the history of humankind, and they were good and just. You are a true leader. You've nursed your boys. Now it's time to lead."

The pressure released and Nonna hobbled away, her silk robes ruffling in the cool Mediterranean breeze like the glamorous old movie star she was, as if she hadn't just laid a great pearl of wisdom at my feet.

Rosemary sent for Coronis in case we needed her healing ability, and we jogged through the winding streets to meet her out front of the basilica. She looked equal parts apprehensive and excited, which summed up how I felt.

"Are you ready to change your life?" she asked.

"Is anyone?"

"I think it's beyond brave," Rosemary said. She stepped forward and wrapped the pelt around my shoulders. It smelled wild and dangerous. "This should protect you, but if you feel anything menacing, ever, come right back out. We can always find another way to get your siren what she wants."

"What if this is the only way to know what I truly am?"

"Who says this will give you the answer?" Coronis countered. "Maybe the demon siren was lying about triggering your powers."

That was a sobering thought. I pulled the lion skin closer and let Rosemary pin it at the hollow in my throat. "Let's find out, eh?" she said gently. She pulled the magnificent mane of the pelt over my head so that I was completely covered.

I wished my friends go could inside with me, but I knew this was something I had to do alone. With one hesitant foot, I went to the door. There was a slight pulse, heavy and dense, but with a single push I passed to the other side. It almost felt like passing through a wall of Jell-O, but once I got through, the pressure on all sides relaxed. Still, I didn't take off the fur.

I went straight to the crypt. I had no idea where or what would trigger my powers, but it was the only place I hadn't been yet. It was also the most protected, so it seemed like a good place to start. I wanted this so badly. To know that I was different. That all of those people were wrong about me. That I could still be destined for great things, even in this middle part of my life.

I took out a flashlight and shined it into the dark entrance of the crypt. Cracked stone steps led downwards, and cobwebs filled the edges. I could already feel the cold seeping up from the damp earth. Resisting the urge to shiver, I took a first tentative step. Then another. I could do this.

The stairs were uneven, and each stone had a little sunken impression from hundreds of years of padding feet. It made me wonder whose footsteps I was following in.

Despite the eeriness, the crypt felt a little sterile the deeper I got. No rodents or any other life existed down here. When I reached the bottom, I pulled Marco's fur around me tighter, the bitter cold making my teeth chatter and goosebumps speckle my arms. This place reeked of ancient magic.

I swept my light around the small space. Except for the sealed tombs, it was empty and deserted. There was a tiny wooden door that looked like it had been built for gnomes in the far corner. I knelt and yanked on the iron ring.

Nothing happened.

I tugged a few more times, a whisper suffusing the air around me like cigarette smoke. Without articulating a word, it told me I was getting close. I could feel the air change, the pressure beginning to build around me. My eardrums popped, but still the door wouldn't budge.

I knew it was the island fighting me, trying to keep me from my future, so I pushed on. Even inside my protection, the pressure was nearly unbearable, bringing me to my knees. In a final effort, I crashed into the door with my shoulder and screamed, "You cannot stop me!"

To my amazement, the door creaked on its hinges and swung open. Instantly, the pressure in the room receded, and I fell forward into a dark set of tunnels.

From here, I had to crawl. The stone was cold and hard on my hands and knees, and I winced at the pain. I was going to have bruises covering them tomorrow. I'd better come out of here with something impressive. Something mind-bending.

I crawled at least thirty feet before reaching a fork in the tunnel. My head swung left and right. I closed my eyes, opening my senses. In all my years of yoga and meditation, I'd always been overwhelmed by a million things, never achieving that coveted blankness. Now, I let myself sink into the quiet of the tunnel. I could hear moisture dripping slowly to my right. I could smell the tang of ancient magic. I could feel the chill. Regardless of what happened, being on Aradia had helped me regain peace. I didn't need Jim to survive. I survived before him and I would after him.

So which way?

I reached my arm out to each fork. The left felt colder, and my gut told me it was that way, whatever I was seeking. So I went left.

The descent was steeper, leading deeper into the earth. I groped forward as sensations of fear and excitement grew with each foot.

The path ended at another door, and my hand hovered over the latch. This was it. Only this door stood between my old life and my new one. I knew it as well as I knew every word in my favorite quote by the French writer, Anaïs Nin. *"Life shrinks or expands in proportion to one's courage."*

With a deep breath, I shoved the door open. A jolt went through me as I staggered into a small room. Everything was dark, and it felt as if all sound here was swallowed. Somehow I knew it had kept itself hidden by absorbing all light and noise. Until my arrival.

My flashlight spread a warm, yellow glow over everything. It was all stone, except for a huge sarcophagus in the middle of the room. I had to cover my mouth with my hand to suppress the yelp of surprise.

I wasn't alone.

A man was on a marble slab. He had a shroud covering his lower half and his arms crossed over his chest, but I could still see his face. He was terrifyingly beautiful. An unnatural beauty that felt like a gut punch every time I looked at him, almost as if his angular lines, high cheekbones, and sharp jaw had been carved from poisoned marble. The toasted nut color of his skin looked like it had been imbued by the desert itself, and black hieroglyphs curled softly up and down his biceps. I knew exactly who it was. The man from my Emerald Tablet vision.

Thoth.

"What am I supposed to do?" I muttered, walking around the slab. His eyes were closed, but if I bent closely, I could see his eyeballs moving underneath. Just like the vision. He was trying to wake up. I had the feeling he'd been trying to wake up for thousands of years. A wash of emotions flooded me.

A dying god, preserved on the island.

War, loss, death. More to come.

Twisting heartbreak. Anger. All-consuming, all-encompassing.

I wrenched back. Were those his thoughts? Or did they belong to the Wandering Goddess? Smoke and debris had covered a field of bodies. Thoth blamed someone. He was waiting for something, too.

With one look, I knew I did not want him awake. Coronis was right about the gods. They were too vengeful and much too dangerous for our world.

Panic began to rise in my chest. I was worried my presence would somehow pull him from his sleep. And then what? I had to fight an undead god? No thank you. The hieroglyphs caught my eye. They were shifting on his skin. Dissolving into different shapes and rearranging themselves into more intricate patterns. I had no idea what they said, and no way to find out. My fingers itched to trace them. It was more like a compulsion.

With nothing else to go on, I stretched out—and immediately was thrown against the crypt's stone walls. Chunks of rock rained down on me as a halo of brilliant white light blasted through the chamber.

Once again, I collapsed to my knees, and Marco's fur slid from my shoulders. "No!" I lunged for it, but a blue light arced from Thoth's chest toward the only living thing in the chamber. Me.

It lanced inside, and I went spread-eagle; the darkness surrounded my senses like I was under a cold, black sea. When I tried to scream, it came out gurgled and impotent.

My nerves felt exposed and fried as the surge continued. It crackled out through my limbs, igniting my senses. A force began to build in the center of my chest. I couldn't tell how long it lasted, only that it was over when I opened my eyes and found myself heaving on the ground. Every breath felt precious and hard-won.

Then I remembered.

Thoth.

I jumped to my feet, wobbly and unsteady, as if I'd paid extra to have that Slavic gym trainer kick my butt all over again. I'd gone to her a few years ago in an attempt to get my pre-twins body back. While she was terrifying, I'd take her "plank, you little fool!" over this feeling any day.

Was he awake? Was he going to kill me?

But Thoth was still asleep, his eyes spinning erratically in their sockets.

I tried taking a few steps, but my lightheadedness threatened to pull me under again. I cursed whatever this was. Was it power? Because it felt more like ineptitude.

Although, if I concentrated, I could almost trace the path of my veins and feel the blood pulsing in them. It felt frenetic. Chaotic energy throbbed across the surface of my skin and hummed in my head. I couldn't even begin to understand it, let alone access it, but it didn't matter. Right now, I needed to get out. I couldn't stand one more minute by Thoth.

With painfully slow movements, I slid across the cold stone floor, working my way through the tunnel with frequent stops for rest. I had to drag Marco's hide behind me, and it left tufts of fur in my wake.

Finally, the air began to taste cleaner, and I could smell incense above me. I was close. It took all of my energy to pull myself through the tiny door, up the stairs of the crypt, and down the row of pews.

Coronis and Rosemary stood at the entrance, banging against an invisible wall that prevented them from entering. Their faces were torn with concern, and my heart surged.

"What happened?" they asked in unison, as I staggered out.

"I'm fine," I promised, lying only a little so they wouldn't worry. "Just woozy."

They hooked me under my arms and pulled me into the evening sun to sit on the steps. "We heard an explosion and the basilica shook, but we couldn't get in."

"Something happened," I said, "but I have no idea what."

Coronis took my pulse and checked me over for burns

or contusions. "You don't know if your powers were awakened?"

"I think they were, but I don't know what it means. All I know is that my senses feel heightened."

Now that I was outside, I realized I had a pounding headache, as if the intensity of the sounds and smells around me were more than my mind could bear. It also felt as if sand had replaced my blood. Lifting my arms suddenly became an Olympic sport. I was bone-weary and overwhelmed. All I wanted was my bed and a bottle of aspirin.

Coronis sensed my pain. "There, there. Let me relieve some of the pressure." Her cool fingers felt like a balm on my fiery skin.

"Thank you," I told her gratefully. "Did you know there's someone down there?"

They both jumped at that.

"Not just someone, either. A god. Thoth."

"Are you quite sure, Ava?"

I ran my fingers over my arm. "He had hieroglyphs all over his body. They changed. He lay so still and silent, but his eyes were moving despite being shut."

"But why do you think he's a god?" Coronis asked.

"Gut feeling," I said. It was true. In my gut, I knew he was the god that threatened the Wandering Goddess. "He's waiting for something. Or he's trapped. I'm not really sure."

Rosemary helped me to my feet. "Oh, dear. I don't like this at all."

"Me neither," Coronis said. "But thankfully he's still unconscious. We'll continue monitoring the basilica to make sure no one accidentally wakes him up."

"Good idea," I said. "And now, apparently, I have to get ready for a date."

Chapter Twenty-One

LUCA PICKED me up at precisely eight p.m. If he'd arrived a few minutes earlier, he would have witnessed my mad dash to take a shower, tame my hair, and apply my makeup in a way that covered my bruises without making me look like a hooker.

My hair had become a routine in and of itself these days. Honestly, it was getting a little out of control. I still had no idea what it meant. What did being really hairy have to do with powers? Maybe I was some type of animal, like Marco. Maybe that's why I got along so well with Rosemary and Coronis. As for powers? If falling asleep at the speed of sound was one, then yeah, I had powers.

"*Bocca al lupo*," Tiberius whispered as he slipped away.

"What does that mean?"

"It's Italian for good luck. Like break a leg, but it means 'in the mouth of a wolf'. You're supposed to say *crepi* back."

"*Crepi*. What's that mean?"

"Let it die."

I did a double-take as Luca knocked on the door three times. "You guys are dark."

Tiberius shrugged, his whiskers twitching excitedly, and gestured a paw at the door. I hurried to open it, saying a prayer under my breath: *Please let my unknown and potentially uncontrollable powers stay put during this date.* Not that I believed I was that powerful, but the last thing I needed was to turn into a giant ostrich during dinner.

Luca stood outside wearing a linen charcoal suit and holding a single pink flower. He extended it toward me, which I found sweet. Luca didn't need flashiness.

"Thank you," I breathed in its perfume. "That's very thoughtful."

"I'm a little out of practice, but its beauty was nearly unrivaled," Luca said in his deep baritone, which was when my insides turned into a warm, fluttering mess.

I grabbed a light jacket and my purse and called to the kitchen, "Nonna, I'll be back later."

Aurick poked his head around the corner. "Ah, Ava. Have a good time. I'll see you at breakfast." To Luca, he gave a curt nod.

Luca advanced a step, his hand extended. They shook, but I could see their knuckles whitening as the handshake lasted a little longer than strictly necessary, each one taking in the other's measure. While Luca was tall, Aurick still towered over him. Yet, where Aurick was lean and light, Luca's dark frame was swathed in muscles and stubble.

I glanced between the two men. Two perfect models of the male species. What woman wouldn't be a little giddy? I had no remorse. "Of course, Aurick. I'm sure Luca is the perfect gentleman."

Luca, for his part, remained unruffled. He held the door for me and helped me with my helmet again, his fingers softly touching the underside of my chin as he clicked it into place. I twirled the flower into a button hook on my purse and resisted the urge to glance back at the villa's windows to see if Aurick was watching.

I succeeded, but barely.

Luca slung a leg over his own Vespa, like he was straddling a Harley. It was as hot as his hard-earned wrinkles around his eyes and mouth. "To town?" he asked.

I nodded and we were off. If you had told me a month ago, as I made yet another dinner salad to go with pasta and red sauce, that I'd be headed for divorce, going on a date with a hunky Italian man, and living in a villa with an ancient crone, I would have choked on a crouton and died laughing. Thankfully that didn't happen so I could enjoy this.

It felt like the world was opening up to me. Finally, I could choose my own destiny. There was no denying that I had felt mostly alone in my old life, especially when the twins grew older and made their own friends. Here, I was submersed in new people and new possibilities. That alone was worth the price of admission.

Once we arrived in town, we parked our rides in front of Marco's taverna. "Would you like to walk a little before dinner?" Luca asked. "I always find it helps with my appetite."

"Sure. Why not?" I said, praying nothing weird would happen, like attracting a hive of bees.

The square was quietly busy. Plenty of people went about their business, grabbing sandwiches, which I found out were calf's liver, and bottles of wine from Marco for their own family dinners. There was a butcher's shop and a cheesemonger that I hadn't visited yet, and a shop dedicated to honey.

"What's your stance on pigeons?" I asked as we

watched the birds take flight, cooing their songs against a rosy, sun-drenched backdrop.

Luca raised an eyebrow. "Pigeons?"

"You know. Avian masters of the sky or rats with wings? It's a very important debate that can reveal a lot about a person."

"This feels like a trap."

"I'll go first if it helps. They're beautifully misunderstood creatures that delivered messages during World War II. Now you go. Don't make a mistake." I smiled and poked him in the ribs with an elbow.

"Ah. So, saying they're a public health hazard is probably not what you're looking for."

"To each his own." I had a sudden surge of longing for home. My boys loved history. They used to enjoy dragging us to museums, as if they were the parents. The natural history museum with dinosaur bones was their favorite, but a good medieval knight and armory exhibit always lit up their eyes, too.

Luca sensed the change. He stopped in front of Marco's taverna and faced me with scrunched eyebrows. "What's the matter, Ava?"

I tried waving it away and steeling myself. This was my first date in decades. Even if Luca wasn't marriage material and even if I didn't plan on going on a second, I still wanted to enjoy my first. "I just miss my boys. So, what do you think Marco is serving tonight? I adore his pasta."

"Don't do that."

"What exactly am I doing?" Anger riled within, waking the sleeping beast of magic. It lifted its head to sniff the air and decide what to do.

"Pretending you're fine when you're obviously not."

And just like that, the beast wound down, putting its head between its paws. Luca was unexpected, like a dark chocolate truffle with layers of nougat and cream inside. Something I'd like to savor.

"Would you like to try calling again? It's still early afternoon in the States."

"Honestly, it's okay. I can try tomorrow," I said, half-heartedly. Yes, yes I did want to call them.

"Let's go up to my apartment." He looked sideways at me. "Sorry, that sounded like an indecent proposition. I only meant to use the phone."

I patted his pleasantly firm bicep. "It's fine. I knew what you meant. To be honest, I would love that. Thank you for being so thoughtful."

When we arrived at his apartment, Luca took my jacket and purse as I went to dial, anticipation surging through my whole body. For some reason, I knew this time would work.

I drummed my fingers on Luca's wooden table to release some of the tension. And then my heart jumped out of my throat when I heard their voices, only to be replaced by disappointment.

"You've reached Josh and Jacob Longsworth."

I began to leave another short message about missing and loving them when the line clicked to life.

"Mom?"

I almost dropped the phone I was so excited. "Josh? Oh my God, Josh!" It was a tsunami. I started bawling at that one precious word. *Mom.*

"Mom? What's wrong?" Josh asked, alarmed. "We've been trying to call you back, but your phone never works." He was always my sweet snuggler. I used to have to talk him into going to kindergarten by giving him kisses on his palms and putting them in his pockets. "That way, you can pull out a kiss whenever you need it," I told the sniffling little boy. And now he was a man. A man who didn't need me anymore. Thank God he had to call me his mom forever.

"Nothing." I choked up my tears, trying to pat my cheeks dry so my makeup wouldn't run. "I don't get service here, but I miss you. I have a million questions, but we probably shouldn't talk long. I doubt the island has an international plan."

"Are you seriously in Italy?" he asked. "Hang on, Jacob's here."

I heard shuffling as they put the phone between them. "Hey, Mom!"

"Jacob, I miss you both so much! Yes, I'm in Italy. I don't know if you've spoken to your father or not?"

Jacob snorted. "He sent us a text message to let us know you were getting divorced. He even put an emoji. It was the one with a freezing, blue face covered in ice to describe you."

"When we texted him back," Josh added, "saying he needed to fix things with you, he told us he had already moved on."

Anger buzzed at my fingertips again. I suppressed it as best I could. The last thing I needed was to blow up Luca's apartment or fry the islanders only source of communication to the outside world. "I'm sorry you had to hear it that way, but everything will be fine. Your college tuition will not be touched, and I'm enjoying a little vacation. Aradia is a small island off the coast of Italy, and boys, you will love it! What do you think about flying here for Thanksgiving break? As long as you don't have exams that week."

"That sounds awesome," Josh said. "We don't have a home to go back to anyway."

"Of course, you do," I said.

"No way," they replied in unison.

"I understand you're mad. I am too, but he's still your father."

"I don't know why you stayed with Dad as long as you did," Jacob said.

I rubbed my temple with my free hand. "Marriage is… complicated."

Jacob snorted. "Not really. You love each other or you don't, the end."

Oh, sweet, naïve boy. Never change. "Well, don't worry about anything. I promise it will be fine. Now tell me how classes are going? Do you like them? Have you decided on a major?"

We talked for a few more minutes about dorm life. Mundane instances of schedules and communal showers made me feel like I was part of their lives, even if deep down, I was still fuming at Jim.

When I hung up, I saw Luca watching me over a steaming mug of something. He handed me a second one. "Tea?"

"Sure." I let the warmth seep into my palms and heal me little by little.

"You are a great mother," Luca told me solemnly.

"Thank you. It doesn't always feel that way in the moment. In fact, it feels more like I'm messing everything up, and it's the highest stakes game of my life, because when I mess up, it affects these two precious little lives that had no say in being born."

"I'm sure they are fine, young men. They must be to worry about their mother."

"Thank you," I said again, and I meant it.

Out of the corner of my eye, I saw the potted plant near the landline. Where it had once been brown and dying, it was now vibrant, even glowing, with new vines and leaves unfurling in front of me. Oh no! I must have done something to it when I got upset.

I slid in front of it so Luca wouldn't notice, my panic expanding as quickly as the plant vines. Was that my new super power? Sprucing up plants?

Desperately, I looked around for a distraction. "Oh, what's that?" I asked, pointing to a glass jar half-hidden behind a pile of books on a shelf. From what I could see, it had moss growing on its lid and something sparkling on the inside.

Luca leapt up and covered it with an apologetic look. "Ah, that's my wife's. I didn't realize it was out."

Tenderness stabbed through me. "Oh, I'm sorry. I had no idea. It's just so magical." I noticed he used the present tense, like he truly couldn't let her die.

Luca came closer, putting his rough, calloused hand on my cheek. He tilted my chin up to meet his. "It is I who am sorry. I didn't mean to make you feel guilty. In fact, that's the furthest thing from my desires."

When Luca leaned down, I felt that moment of suspension—like the one before a fall where your body dreads and anticipates the feeling all in the same hot swoop. Then his lips were on mine, and I found myself wanting to kiss him back. My arms went around his neck as his hands slid into my hair, deepening the kiss. The butterflies in my stomach took flight with fully unfurled wings, flapping insistently as my heart thudded against my chest. Luca's kisses became stronger, more persistent, and I felt as if I'd never been properly kissed before.

"Ava!"

"Ava, where are you?"

We broke apart, looking as guilty as my teens with their bedroom door closed and a girl inside. I went to the window and threw it open to see both Rosemary and

Coronis calling my name in the street, their hands cupped around their mouths.

"What's going on?" I waved.

They both looked up. If they were surprised by my presence inside Luca's apartment, they didn't let it show. "There you are!" Rosemary cried, relief suffusing her voice. "I'm sorry to interrupt you, but Thessaly needs us."

Chapter Twenty-Two

I MADE my apologies to Luca, saying a friend needed me. Not exactly a lie, but definitely a stretch. Then I promised to reschedule—Another date? Yes, please!—and sprinted out of his apartment. The moment we turned the corner, I let Rosemary carry me to the ocean as a harpy.

"You are a strong, independent woman," I kept muttering to myself, over and over. "One amazing kiss will not undo you. Two might, though, so watch it."

"What are you saying?" Rosemary called over the wind.

"Nothing!"

They'd already given me a sideways look when I came outside, my hair mussed and my lips swollen.

Rosemary gently lowered me onto Thessaly's rock, but I still slipped and had to catch myself.

Coronis shifted back into a human and joined us, her black feathers morphing into her ice white bob. "Sorry, darling. I hope we didn't disturb you and Luca?"

"It's fine," I said, feeling my cheeks grow warm. "He let me use his phone."

"Of course, he did."

"No, really. I finally got through to my boys, too."

"Darling, that's wonderful! I hope they're both well?"

I nodded, the warmth now spreading through my body at the thought of them. I was so glad they had each other. At least they wouldn't have to go through life alone. "Okay, who's going to tell me what's going on?"

"Once you came out of the basilica, we realized we could get inside," Coronis explained. "It's possible you broke the curse Aradia was keeping over it."

Rosemary looked thoughtful. "Or maybe it didn't matter anymore. Once Ava got in and received her powers, what use did Aradia have keeping it locked? The island could have stopped on its own."

"Who knows?" I said. "Either way, you got in. Then what?"

"We were able to see the old manuscripts. I mean, the really old ones. In languages we'd never seen before because they belonged to the gods."

"So how did you read them?" I asked.

"Nonna," they said together.

"Tiberius was able to translate enough to learn that the curse that holds Thessaly could be undone by the woman who was a wolf."

"Do you mean like a wolf-shifter? Is there someone like that on the island?"

The women exchanged glances. I didn't think I liked where this was going. My hand went automatically to the huge mane of hair that wouldn't stop growing. I would have killed for this in my twenties after the boys. It had started falling out in clumps the minute I stopped nursing them and never quite recovered its luster. But now? It curled down my shoulders like I was taking super illegal Russian collagen pills.

Before I could question them further, a figure rose from the waves, and ripples expanded out around Thessaly as she broke the surface, moonlight tinting her blue hair silver.

"Have you found something?" she asked. She was trying to act unaffected, but I could feel an undercurrent of excitement. Fish swirled in the eddies around her and breached the water in their jumps.

"We have," Coronis said tentatively.

"What are you waiting for then? Free me!"

"What are our assurances that you won't try to kill us the moment we do?" Coronis asked reasonably.

"Because I could kill you now, yet I don't."

"Only because you want something."

The siren smiled. The blue of her lips peeled back to reveal her small, sharpened teeth. "Despite what the gods wanted me to be, I am not a murderer. I have resisted for hundreds of years. All I want now is to walk on the earth, to feel the dirt between my toes, to pick a grape from the vine, and let the heat of the sun warm my skin." She held out her forearm. "Feel me."

I caught the other women's eyes. She certainly sounded persuasive, and I remembered how cold she'd felt when she'd held me the last time.

Lightly, I touched her arm and instantly jerked back my hand, curling my fingers into my chest. "Your touch is ice."

"Because my blood is sluggish. I want to feel heat again. I want to run, to dance, to sweat. Is that so wrong?"

I couldn't imagine being trapped in the orbit of a little island in the Mediterranean, unable to get warm. It was a spectacularly unjust punishment. But it was still a punishment.

"What did you do to call the wrath of the gods?" I asked.

"What does any woman do to call the wrath of the gods?" she responded. "I fell in love."

"With a man?" I asked.

"A mortal, yes," Thessaly allowed. "He died centuries ago and still I pay the price."

We all let that sit with us for a moment. If she wasn't lying, it didn't seem fair that Thessaly would have to pay this price for eternity since the gods were banished.

"You have to swear on the gods that you will not betray us," Rosemary demanded.

"I swear it on the old gods and the new."

I shrugged. "Good enough for me. What do we do next?"

"Darling, it's what do *you* do next."

Thessaly's eyes roved up and down my body at Rosemary's words. "Ah. Something has changed. You've done the impossible."

I put a hand to my chest and I could feel my heart beat speeding up. "Me? Can you sense what it is?"

"You still do not know?" she asked. "It's not insignificant. Use it. Use it on me."

"I would if I knew what exactly IT is. At Luca's, I brought his dying plant back to life. What does that make me?"

"A nurturer. But not by nature. You were never meant to be what you are. You were cursed."

"What does that have to do with a wolf?"

"Not any wolf. You're the She-Wolf of legend."

"She-Wolf?" I quipped. "Any relation to She-Ra?"

Everyone stared at me confused, apparently having missed the coolest 80s show ever. "No," Thessaly said.

"She was the mythical mother of the twins Romulus and Remus. Boys fated to fight. Feral children."

Little images floated into my mind.

Two perfect little human boys, curled around my shaggy belly, full of warm milk to keep away the chill of a Roman night in the wild-strewn seven hills. Their wriggling little bodies suckled until they slept sated. The chafing of raw nipples.

I remembered my own belly, heavy with my twins. They were constantly twisting and squirming in my womb, jockeying for position, which meant I was constantly fixated on whether they were doomed to hate each other after being so combative. Jim said I was overthinking it. That I couldn't decide their entire future based on how often they moved in my belly. He was proud they were feisty. Maybe he was right, but he still managed to diminish my feelings on a constant basis when I needed to be supported and heard, to have my emotions validated, so I wouldn't feel so very alone. I used to cradle my stomach and croon lullabies, promising I would love them forever.

"So, let me get this straight. You think, because I have twin boys, that I'm the mythical She-Wolf of Rome? The mother of the twins Romulus and Remus."

"Yes," Thessaly said, a little too matter-of-factly for my taste. Demon or not, I expected a piece of information like that to be delivered with a little more delicacy.

"First off," I began, "my boys were wild, but hardly feral. I always made sure they washed behind their ears and put their dishes away. We had the sex talk multiple times, not just once. They are respectful, upstanding, young men." Sure, they got into their share of trouble. Perhaps more than their share, but that was because there were two of them. "They're not feral," I repeated.

"Your sons are not Romulus and Remus," Thessaly

said. "Do not worry about that. Focus on finding that nurturing energy of the mother wolf, and free me."

Good Lord, this siren had a one-track mind. Could I not stop for a few minutes to catch my breath? How could I have been a freaking wolf thousands of years ago? I didn't think I had any particular affinity for the moon or red meat. I guess I did enjoy steak and wild boar Bolognese more than most, but cooked. Always cooked. Okay, except for beef tartare. I got that once on my birthday at a steak house. Jim hated the texture, but I thought it was magnificent.

Oh no. I was a wolf.

"Wait." I held up a hand. "You said something about a curse?"

"Do not bother asking me more. I have no answers. Willingly or not."

"Let's get this going," Coronis snapped. "I'm freezing. And frankly, I still don't trust you. The sooner you're gone, the better."

"Haughty words from a crow shifter."

"Okay," I stepped between them, referee-like. "What do I do?"

"It's something to do with the moon," Rosemary said. "You have an affinity with it due to your wolf nature—and so does the siren."

I felt so normal, so insignificant, it was hard to imagine I was somehow harboring magic strong enough to break a god's curse. "How did you know it was me?" I asked faintly.

Rosemary trailed a finger down my shoulder blade, and my head turned to follow. "Holy... What is that?" I asked, twisting back and forth, trying to get a better view of the huge tattoo unfurled across my upper back in intricate, gossamer lines.

"We saw that in a manuscript."

My breath hitched. "No."

They nodded. "And we'd noticed it the other night at apertivo hour."

"I've never seen this in my life," I promised, trying to feel the lines with my fingers. It seemed to glow in the dark. A kohl-lined eye on the left, a kohl-lined eye on the right. A cobra wrapped around a solar disc in the middle. But it didn't make any sense. "If I'm a wolf with a moon affinity, can anyone tell me why this is a sun?"

Only the sound of the waves responded to my question.

"Great," I muttered.

"Others will come for you," Thessaly warned. "They may propose marriage or simply try to take what they want from you. Heirs to build the next empire."

A deep, biting, cold fear scrabbled at my throat. "I already have twin boys. Does that mean they're in danger?"

Coronis took a step back, the thought actually staggering her. "Yes, possibly. If anyone were to find out you already had twins, they might want to use them or kill them to breed their own children with you."

I felt like I'd somersaulted and landed wrong on my neck. Nausea swept through me. "I need to go to them. I need to protect them."

Rosemary and Coronis came and squeezed both of my hands. "Darling, perhaps they are safest without you nearby? Nobody knows you exist yet."

Coronis added, "And one of us can do a spell of protection on them. To shield them from other supernatural beings ever finding them. Would that help?"

The tight feeling around my heart refused to let go. I doubted anything other than standing guard over their beds while they slept would help. But what choice did I have? I nodded my assent. "Can you do it right now?"

"As soon as we're done here," Coronis promised.

I rubbed my hands together, my heart beat pulsing through my body at the thought of my boys in danger.

Thessaly, however, was focused on one thing. "What are you waiting for?" she demanded.

"I don't know. Directions, perhaps. Should I touch you or something?"

Thessaly frowned. "That doesn't feel auspicious."

"None of this does, sister. Here, let me touch your forehead or something." I reached out and placed my palm on her cheek. For a second, nothing happened, then the clouds shifted and a sliver of moonlight pierced my skin, covering me in quicksilver.

I let out a scream and Thessaly's body fused to mine. It was like touching a glacier. The solar disc blazed white hot across my back, and raw magic steamed into the night air. I thought I saw Rosemary flash into a harpy to catch me as I fell, my eyelids fluttering closed.

And then I felt nothing.

Chapter Twenty-Three

SOMETHING SMELLED WARM.

I sniffed the air, my snout rising. I could sense the pulsing of blood beneath skin. Heat. A rabbit? Moving at a gentle lope, my distended belly swayed from my recent litter. Everything ached. My udders dripped milk, but it wasn't enough. My pups had died one by one. If I was human, I might have thought it was divine interference. Instead, I had howled. My mournful cries echoed in the hills, but my mate never answered.

When the flood waters receded, they left behind rotted plant debris and silted muck on the banks of the hill. A fig tree rose at the edge of the water. I went closer. Caught in its roots was a wicker basket. The warmth was inside. I nosed it, shaking the contents. Screeches poured out, and while I was a predator first, I was oddly tired. So, I poked my nose inside the squirming mess. A fist grabbed me and clenched with a fierceness I wasn't expecting.

Humans. Little brutes. So helpless and hungry. Only the maternal instinct made my body pause. The human babes could suckle and give me relief. I took the wicker handles between my teeth and trotted back to my cave.

They were voracious and as greedy as my pups should have been.

I licked them for hours, pleased with this bounty, not knowing it was the gods who orchestrated it.

I didn't understand when a shining man in robes stood before me, as feral as my mate. My hackles rose and I shrunk back, whimpering while the boys slept behind me. They were toddlers now, nourished on nuts and berries along with my milk.

The man spoke. "Maternal compassion. Ferocious violence. The She-Wolf is a slippery creature. You have always been impossible to cage. So you will embody a lupa, *and I will always know where you are."*

He spat on the ground and left.

The boys woke during my transformation. They sobbed giant tears, startling a human couple walking nearby. The humans grabbed my babes to their breast and ran as I writhed on the ground. I never suckled them again. Later, after I became accustomed to walking on two feet and slipping in the shadows in my new form, I hunted them until I found their scent and the men they'd become. I watched them from afar.

Now, they bared their teeth, their feral nature forever simmering at the surface. My milk had made them ferocious opponents on and off the battlefield. I spied on them as they stormed an agora and overthrew a murderous king, proudly watching the way their swords shone in the sun, battling in rhythm with each other. And, I'd finally learned who they were. Romulus and Remus, descendants of a man named Aeneas. Two boys sent to die in that flooded wicker basket.

Still, I only watched.

Now, my boys were at war again—but with each other.

"You only saw six vultures on your hill. Twelve of the birds circled my hill," Romulus said. His jaw ticked as he clenched it tighter around his lie. "This is where we should build our city."

Remus smiled. "Yes, brother. I only saw six, but I saw them before you did. That means the gods wish us to build on my hill."

Romulus struck his spade in the dirt where it splintered from his brute force. "You are wrong."

"I'm the eldest," Remus said, a smile still on his face. The babe who always snuggled the closest on cold nights. The one who had seen six vultures first, where Romulus had seen none.

Romulus's face twisted in rage. "That does not mean the gods favor you."

"It does. We build on the Aventine Hill."

Romulus took his broken spade and knelt to dig. "No. I will build my walls on the Palatine."

I watched, too afraid to interfere. My speech was stilted when I attempted to use it at all, and my clothes, stolen from shepherds and farmers, were patched together. I never found a pack, and I was not fit to be around humans. The boys I'd suckled would recoil in horror at my gnarled hair and sharp nails with dirt crusted under them. They wouldn't understand. I barely understood it myself. Human. I was human.

So I watched as Romulus dug his trenches and built his walls. They were pathetic walls. Remus climbed the Palatine to taunt him. He should have known his brother better.

"You are going to build a shining white city with this?" Remus laughed. He stepped over the haphazard stones, back and forth. "Enemies will have no trouble."

I saw the spade hurtling toward his head, but I was powerless, not nearly as fast in human form. Remus crumpled, blood trickling from his brow. I howled like I hadn't howled in decades. Years of my torment loosened upon the hills.

I ran without waiting, but it was only a few hours before an acrid smell blanketed the seven hills. Remus's funeral pyre spiraled biting smoke as an offering to the gods above while his blood soaked Rome's very foundation. Of course, Romulus had named it after himself.

I wanted to live the rest of my days in my cave. I wanted to die there, so I did.

It took seven hundred years to finally learn that lupa meant both a beastly wolf and a human whore in the language of the Romans, and that it was my curse.

Chapter Twenty-Four

I WOKE up with a chipmunk curled around my neck, Tiberius's tail tickling the little hairs in my nose. I sneezed fur, and black feathers went flying as a large crow surged upwards and shifted into Coronis.

"She's awake!" she cawed to the rest of the house.

I barely had time to take in my surroundings before Nonna crashed into my room. "Mamma!" she cried, hobbling over to give me a hug.

Even Aurick looked worried. "Coronis healed you as best she could, but your back was burned pretty badly. How do you feel?" he asked.

It was then that I felt that rubbery feeling of a half-healed burn covering a third of my back. I winced as I moved. Everything hurt. "Like a crumpled aluminum can that's been continuously rolled over on the freeway."

Aurick smiled. "At least you kept your sense of humor."

I'd noticed around my mid-thirties that when I woke up, my joints hurt until I cracked them. Fingers first, then wrists and ankles. Once I'd swung my legs over my bed and stood, I'd lean on each leg and crack my hips. Jim thought it was loud and weird, but I couldn't start my day otherwise. I had a feeling my entire body was going to be one big painful joint that needed cracking if I got out of bed now.

"That must have been some magic," he continued, an eyebrow raised.

"Must have," Coronis spoke for me as I gaped, still feeling woozy and out of it. Memories of my life as the She-Wolf had assaulted me, making my sleep feel less than restorative.

"Aurick, why don't we go into town and tell Rosemary the good news? We'll grab an espresso. Darling?" Coronis turned to me. "Would you like me to bring you back anything?"

Nonna patted my arm, her cold, veiny hands feeling strangely comforting. "I've got everything she needs. You two go tell Rosemary the good news."

Sunlight filtered in dappled golds across Nonna's handmade bedspread. She'd refilled my vase with wildflowers and left a glass of water next to my bed. I gulped it down, my tongue feeling like I'd licked Thessaly's rock. "What happened?" I asked faintly.

"You funneled god magic, Mamma." Nonna tutted, tucking the sheets in more firmly around me.

"I did?"

"*Sì*, you silly thing. But you survived."

"And Thessaly?"

"Sleeping in the spare bedroom."

I wanted to go talk to her, but I could barely grip the glass cup without dropping it. "Is she okay?"

"*Sì*. Don't worry. Just relax."

I nodded slowly, then bolted up. "My boys! Did Coronis put a protection spell on them?"

Nonna patted my hand. "They are safe. Do not worry

about them. I saw to it myself, astral projecting to their location." Her eyes glowed for a moment, then she laughed. "They are quite messy, your boys. Pizza boxes all over. They even made a chair out of them!"

I laughed with her. That sounded about right. The beating of my heart slowed, and I drifted back to sleep.

The next time I woke, it was dark outside, and the clock next to my bed said five a.m. I could have slept longer, but a series of questions had pulled me from my sleep. What had happened to the She-Wolf for those seven-hundred-years? What had she done? Where had she gone? More fundamentally, who was I then and why did I keep coming back cursed? And something else, a bit more subversive. If I'd broken Thessaly's god curse, could I break my own? Would I even want to?

There were too many threads to follow and implications to consider. If I broke my curse—big if—would that turn me back into a simple wolf? What would that mean for my boys? Would they cease to exist?

Tentatively, I rolled my wrists, testing my strength. Everything still hurt, but it didn't make me want to spend the day unconscious. It was my normal morning pain, turned up to an eleven. Like after a night puking with the flu. I swung my legs over and completed my ritual. It was why I'd turned to yoga a few years ago. It got the blood moving and the joints popping in the morning.

After a quick vinyasa flow, I threw on a silk house robe and went to find Thessaly. Talking to her was more important than espresso. Yes, even espresso.

I crept around the villa like an intruder, hoping to catch her alone. The third bedroom was in the attic, and the creak of the treads sounded like gunshots to my ears as I climbed. Finally, I reached her room and knocked softly. "Thessaly? It's Ava. Can I come in?"

Without waiting for a response, I slipped inside and found the ex-siren with one leg slung over the window sill. She turned around, a guilty look on her face. "Ava."

I crossed my arms in full mom mode again. "Were you always planning on escaping or just when you heard my voice?"

Thessaly slowly hauled herself back into the room. Even though she didn't answer, I knew it was the latter because she was only wearing Nonna's complimentary Villa Venus robe, her chiton still clutched in her hands. She smoothed it over a rocking chair.

"Ava, I'm glad you're alive."

"Same, although I wish it didn't hurt so much to be in the land of the living."

"A small price to pay for the truth."

Before she could evade me, I blurted, "Are you a siren still?"

"Yes. I'm a siren. I still have my powers, but they are no longer tied to that rock. I am free to go, to move, to live. I will wither and die in time."

"You're no longer immortal?" I asked, horrified that I'd condemned her to die.

"I knew the cost and I was willing to pay it. No supernatural is immortal. It may take centuries or even millennia, but we all die."

"But not you. Not under your curse."

"No," she allowed. "I was cursed to always remember, whether I wanted to or not. And you? What did you learn about your curse?"

I thought for a second about the god in the cave. As a wolf, it was hard to see and to remember. I couldn't recall his face, only its savageness, so I wasn't sure if it was the same god under the basilica's crypt. Perhaps it was Thoth.

But why would he want to curse a wolf and turn her human?

"I'm not sure," I said. "A god came into my cave when I was nothing but a wolf on the hills of ancient Rome and said he wanted to always be able to find me. So that's weird."

"Indeed." Thessaly's eyes were fierce, no longer mournful. "Since you saved me, I'll help you. With information. The veil around the island is weakening. Evil is coming. Evil is already here."

My hands went clammy, and I had to wipe them on my shirt. "Can you give me a little more to work with? Is it a person? An object?"

"A person," Thessaly confirmed.

"Well?"

"Well what?"

"Who is it?" I asked.

"I don't know. I can only feel their presence. They arrived before you, but the veil is breaking down. The reason so many ghosts are appearing is because of this weakness. More powerful things will come next because of this tear. Aradia is peaceful, but not all supernaturals are."

The slope was indeed slippery. In a little more than a week, I had gone from thinking Nonna was a "spirted" old woman, to believing in ghosts, to suddenly un-cursing sirens. Now, I had to help save an island from a great evil?

Thessaly undid her robe and put on her chiton. I wondered what it was about me that made other women feel comfortable undressing in front of me. "Careful, Ava," Thessaly said as she tied her chiton at her waist. "Someone is using the ghosts."

"Using them? What could someone use from a ghost?" I frowned.

"Necromancers could use them. They don't, not usually, but they could."

Just hearing the word necromancer made me shiver. It sounded evil. "Where are you going to go?" I asked her.

Thessaly gazed at the bright ocean, a smile playing at her lips. "Wherever I want."

WITH ALL OF the hiking and fresh sea air, I was actually starting to see my old body back. While I'd never see pre-pregnancy weight again—those hips had sailed—at least I could feel comfortable in my body again. Forty really was fabulous. I could do this! I could save the island. I was the She-Wolf, after all. Even if I was a cursed wolf in human skin, I had powers.

With my newfound confidence in tow, I found Luca at the bakery and waved to Rosemary. She immediately dropped the espresso handle, which let off a hiss, and came around the marble cake case. Her hug lifted me off my feet.

"Darling, how are you? Coronis said you were awake, but I didn't expect to see you so soon."

"I promise I'll be back at work tomorrow. I've missed it. But right now," I turned to Luca, "I was hoping I could call my boys?" He stood, too, and gave me a kiss on both cheeks in greeting. His rough stubble rubbed deliciously across my skin.

"Ava, I heard you were sick. I'm glad to see you're feeling better. Would you like to call now?"

It was almost one in the afternoon in Italy, which meant it was closer to seven a.m. on the East Coast. I highly doubted the boys were awake willingly, but maybe they rose early for classes. "Yes, please."

It wasn't that I didn't trust Nonna, but hearing their voices would go a long way to calming my nerves. The fresh smell of Rosemary's Bakery followed us into the square. It was a beautifully warm afternoon that could rival St. Louis for fall beauty. I sucked in deep breaths, happy to be outside, happy to be alive.

Luca, on the other hand, looked miserable. Unless that frown was his permanent companion. In fact, now that I thought about it, had I seen him smile on our date?

"Luca," I ventured. "You've been so kind to me. I was wondering if you needed... well, a shoulder to cry on, so to speak? I'm a good listener."

Luca opened his apartment and held the door for me. "Thank you, Ava, but this is my normal face."

I blushed. Caught. "The offer still stands. I'd be happy to help lighten your mental load."

Luca picked up my hand and brushed a kiss across my knuckles. I inhaled sharply at his bold touch. "I will remember that," he said, before leaving me to collect my cool so I could speak to my boys.

It rang twice before Josh answered, sounding groggy and uninspired. "Hello?"

"Josh! I'm sorry, did I wake you? It's Mom."

"Mom, why are you calling so early?"

Even annoyed, it felt good to hear my baby. Images of the transformed She-Wolf watching Romulus and Remus from afar tried to surface, but I focused on the sound of Josh's voice and pushed them away. "I'm sorry, I get the times confused here. I just wanted to see if you needed anything. Are your dining hall cards full or did you already cash them out on snacks?"

"They're fine," Josh said. I heard a *thunk* and an "ouch!" If I had to guess, he'd thrown something hard at his brother to rouse him. "Here, Jacob wants to say hi."

There was grumbling as the phone switched, and Jacob yawned loudly into the receiver. "Mom? What's going on?"

"Nothing. I only wanted to make sure you were fine," I said truthfully. They were alive. They were good. "And to say that I think you should go home for Thanksgiving. I was being selfish wanting you here, but I know you want to catch up with your old friends."

"Mom? We were planning to visit you."

I wiped away a tear. "That's so sweet, but something came up here and it's nothing to worry about, but it's probably for the best if you went to St. Louis." Lies. All lies. "Perhaps we can Skype or set up something for winter break."

"Wow, okay. I need an energy drink to wake up," Jacob said.

Josh added, "We'd rather see you."

"I know. I'd rather see you, too. I just have to figure some things out first. Can I call you next week with more definitive plans?"

"At noon our time," Jacob yelled in the background, already presumably going back to bed.

I laughed, more tears pricking the corners of my eyes. What the hell? Where was my unemotional composure when I needed it? "Talk soon. Love you both. Study hard!"

We hung up and I looked over at Luca who was casually watching me with his arms folded. "Thank you," I said solemnly.

"I enjoy hearing your love for your sons," he said, sounding a little wistful. And that look in his eyes. He was fighting back his own emotions. I didn't want to set a precedent where I called my sons and then made out with men, but our last kiss haunted me. It was intense, practically toe-curling. Was it a fluke or was he just that good?

I moved a step closer and tilted my chin up. Luca

didn't step back. We were inches away, and my pulse fluttered at my neck. An odd groaning noise made me pause, and I wrinkled my nose at a sudden sulfuric scent. "Luca—"

"I think I better see you out," he said, quickly leading me to the door. "My sewer system has a tendency to back up at inopportune moments."

"Oh, okay," I said, embarrassed for us both.

"That's the problem with these medieval towns. Quaint, but their bones are old."

"I'll see you at Marco's tonight I'm sure," I said in the world's most leading statement.

Luca didn't bite. "Ciao, Ava. I'm glad you're feeling better."

When I got back to Villa Venus, Nonna was in the kitchen, braiding garlic. It smelled aggressive. I sat down to help, but my fingers were worthless and she quickly told me to watch and learn.

Hey, I was a boy mom. We didn't do braids. Or maybe it was because I was lost in my thoughts, which swirled as aggressively as the smell of raw garlic. Necromancers, ancient curses, frightened ghosts. It was all there, all connected, but a few dots were still missing.

"Nonna, did you learn anything at the cemetery? Thessaly said something about a necromancer possibly using the ghosts."

Nonna jumped. "Sorry, Mamma. I got tired and never made it. Want to go with me now?"

"Sure. As long as Aradia doesn't try to kill me."

We took some water bottles and headed to the cemetery, the clear October skies melting into a thick mist as we drew closer. The tattoo on my back warmed when we entered the perimeter, but not in an unpleasant or painful way. Rather, like it was reacting to something and letting me know. I wondered when it had appeared. Had it happened the moment I'd flopped onto Aradia's shores, or was it more subtle, inking itself into being over the last week?

We searched the tombstones and urns for signs of life among the dead. "Do you think they were taken?" I asked after we had done a full circle.

"No idea. Wait, something is glowing over there." We crouched low and watched two orbs mingling for a moment before I realized I was about to crash yet another sex party. Nonna chuckled. "Well look at that."

The sound of our voices and our not-so-subtle crouching (as we both creaked every time we knelt), alerted the orbs to our presence. Instantly, they materialized into the Knight and the seventeenth century Italian housewife. No surprise, they were readjusting their clothing like we hadn't just caught them going to second base. Maybe third. I wasn't sure what the bases meant anymore, but I knew where things were heading.

This was getting a little ridiculous, but at least they weren't flickering and turning distorted like the other ghosts.

"Signora, how can we help?" the Knight asked in a voice lacking all of its usual arrogance. Get a man laid—ghost or not—and his whole outlook on life changed.

"We were wondering if you could help us with a ghost problem. Have you two noticed anything odd with your forms? Any pain or disappearing body parts?" I asked.

They shook their heads, and I pretended not to notice that the woman's left breast was peeking out of her rotting dress. "Hm," I thought out loud, "maybe they're protected in this grove. Is it sacred? It's always night here and misty."

"All groves are sacred, so that's possible," Nonna mused.

"You can poke around, right?" the woman asked. "A big, strong Knight like you, that is."

He puffed out his armored chest, rusted and chinked as it was. "Stay here. I will investigate."

He popped back into a blue orb and winked into whatever spectral plane they inhabited. In two seconds, he was back, wheezing and creaking as badly as our knees.

"I'm getting too old for this," he muttered.

"Has your brain rotted as much as your greaves? You shouldn't take the planes so fast," she fussed.

He flapped her away. "Go on woman, I'm fine. I'm fine. Okay, so it's true that ghosts are popping up more frequently, most not even connected to the island. And they disappear just as quickly."

"Why?" I asked.

"Someone is calling to them. Someone with impure intentions."

"Any clues to what those intentions might be?"

"No, but the veil surrounding and protecting Aradia is very weak. Be careful."

I nodded my thanks. "You too. Better stay inside the grove."

The couple drifted off, still making googly eyes at each other with the occasional barb wrapped in velvet.

Ah. Young love.

Chapter Twenty-Five

AFTER SLEEPING for another twelve hours straight, I came into the kitchen to find Tiberius choking on his morning egg. I pounded his back until he spat it out. "You're never going to learn, are you?"

"Why would I?" Tiberius said, popping the egg back in his mouth. "I have you now. By the way, I forgot to ask in all of the excitement. How was your date with Luca?"

"Short."

"Ouch. That bad?"

"No. Just interrupted."

Nonna handed me a cup of espresso. It was spiked with cinnamon and cloves and smelled divine.

"Interrupted?" Nonna asked.

"Thanks to Thessaly. That was the night we un-cursed her." I grabbed a knife and began to butter my toast when a deep voice broke over us. Tiberius fled to the window at the sound.

"*Buongiorno*, Ava."

I looked up to see Aurick immaculately dressed, even at five in the morning. He wore a fitted, navy blue suit with a white shirt and gold tie. "You look wonderful," he said, kissing both of my cheeks. I could smell some sort of cologne. Something rich and full-bodied.

I handed him the tureen of butter. "Thank you."

"*Buongiorno*, Nonna," he called. "This spread looks lovely."

I finished putting jam on my biscuit and handed him that as well.

"Ava, I was wondering if you'd like to get dinner with me tonight?"

My knife clattered to the floor. Aurick swooped to pick it up and hand me a clean one. "I take it that I've shocked you."

"Don't you think she's a little young for you?" Nonna scowled.

"Ava can make up her own mind. Preferably at dinner. Shall I pick you up?" he bowed with a flourish, and I had to admit it made me laugh. He was being theatrical on purpose, and it was such a difference between Jim's indifference and even Luca's gruffness. Maybe it would be good to get out and have fun with different types of men. Even if I never got serious with either of them, it would be beneficial to know what I liked. Or simply to enjoy myself. At any rate, Luca had felt distant. Perhaps that was his way of letting me down easy.

"Why not? It's a date," I told him.

"Why not, indeed," Nonna muttered.

THAT AFTERNOON AFTER MY SHIFT, I made Coronis show me the protection spells around my boys. If anything magical got within a meter of them, she explained, it would trigger an alarm system and crash down protective wards until help could arrive.

It pained me to stay away, but I couldn't risk exposing them before I had mastered my powers, which is why I spent most of my free time trying to access and understand them. My training ground was my room.

I closed my eyes and concentrated on finding the nub of light and nourishing it. A warm, buttery glow blossomed around me. I could feel individual hairs rising along my neck and scalp.

Suddenly, it all sprouted out, like putting a wet finger into an electrical outlet. My eyes popped open, and I practically scared myself in the mirror. Every hair was standing on end, puffed out like an enraged wolf.

I growled in frustration. This was it? I could make vines grow and become a fuzzy ball of hair to scare my enemies. The only ones who would be frightened were my hairdresser and potential boyfriends.

A knock sounded at my door. Aurick!

"Uh, be right there," I called, frantically smoothing down my hair.

"Take your time," he replied easily, as I rummaged on the floor for a comb.

"So sorry, but could you give me ten minutes? I swear, I never do this, but I lost track of time."

"It's fine. Just come out when you're ready."

I sprayed some of Nonna's hairspray circa 1944 over my head and combed it down before finding the outfit Coronis had let me borrow.

A few minutes later, I emerged, breathing heavily as if I had just finished a workout routine. Aurick smiled graciously and offered me his arm. "You look beautiful, Ava."

The night sky was clear and stars sparkled as Aurick

steered us into town, parking in front of Marco's taverna. But instead of heading inside, he led me down one of the back alleyways. I raised my eyebrow. "Do you know something about this island that I don't know?"

Aurick shot me a half-smile that made my legs wobbly. "Wouldn't that be weird?"

"Either that," I mused. "Or you're going to murder me. Just so you know, Rosemary, Coronis, and Nonna all know where I am and are probably tracking me. Marco is part lion. He'll tear you to shreds if you even stare at me wrong."

"Have you always talked this fast? Or is it a learned trait?" he asked, sounding amused.

"Wow. Your romantic game needs some practice."

He snorted. "You were the one that accused me of plotting your murder."

"Right. Well, I readily admit that I'm totally out of practice." It was true. Without Coronis lending me her clothing, I would've been a wreck.

Now, her velvet, ox-blood red dress hugged my curves without revealing too much, and her tan booties gave me a few more inches to bring me up to 5'7. It was still almost a foot shorter than Aurick, but I didn't mind. Being next to him made me feel petite and cute. She finished it off with a black leather jacket I adored.

Aurick opened a little wooden gate that creaked on its hinges. "After you," he bowed.

I folded my arms across my chest. When I noticed little sparks of gold lighting up my fingertips, I quickly uncrossed them and hid them behind my back.

"This is the part where everyone screams for the woman not to go in first."

Aurick let out a guffaw at that. His eyes were twinkling.

"Thank you for showing me such a blind spot in my murder education."

I poked him in the chest, impressed at the thickness. "You're welcome."

We stood expectantly, waiting for each other. Finally, "You're quite serious, aren't you?"

"Like a dead hooker."

Aurick let loose a true laugh for once. "You're different."

"Special. That's what you're supposed to say. So, are you going inside?"

Aurick went first and I followed, feeling my unpredictably wild mother magic sparking up my wrists. Then I gasped. Twinkly lights lit up a grove of lemon trees, and there was a small table with two iron chairs tucked underneath. A bottle of wine sat in a straw base between two candles. This was seriously the most romantic thing I'd ever seen outside of the movies.

I reached up to touch a lemon. It hung heavy, dense with juice, and smelled divine. For a moment, the scent of lemons ricocheted me to that airy bedroom from the memory I had stolen from the Runaway Goddess. I closed my eyes, trying to return to the here and now. *In and out*. When I opened my eyes, Aurick was watching me with those chess-eyes of his.

"I impressed you," he said.

"It's beautiful," I admitted. "And I had no idea it was back here. How did you?"

"I asked Marco for advice."

"Look at you! A real go-getter."

Aurick pulled out my chair and scooted me under, just as Marco appeared with a two-handled ceramic pot of something that smelled deliciously fresh, like the ocean. He placed it on the table and lifted the lid with a flourish.

"Seafood stew with saffron zabaglione. *Buon appetito!*"

"I thought zabaglione was only for sweet desserts?"

"Just replace the sugar with sea salt and saffron and use a dry white wine instead of a sweetened one," Marco winked.

Aurick poured me a glass and held up his own. "To an interesting night."

I clinked with his. "To an interesting toast."

He was trying to figure out what I was, while I was trying to figure out what he was. This should be fun.

We both took a sip, still watching each other over the rims of our glasses. It was a delicious white wine, sharp and full of minerals, that swirled on the tip of my tongue. "Nice choice," I complimented him.

"Thank you." He looked over the steaming bowl of food in an expert appraisal and bade me to lift my plate so he could serve me. I took the opportunity to study him while he was occupied. His light hair had more shades of blonde than a paint store, with a few reddish-gold glints for good measure. His teeth were white and straight—blindingly so. Where he was wrinkled and tired before, now his smoothed skin shone with an inner radiance.

I cleared my throat to keep myself from staring at his soft lips. "So, what brought you to Aradia?"

"Time away. I ended up having to recover from my journey for longer than I anticipated."

"A year?"

He served himself next. "More or less."

"That's quite the nap. It must have been some trip."

Aurick laughed. "I may have secrets, but you, Ava Falcetti, are infinitely more fascinating."

"Little old me?" I laughed it off.

"Yes."

"You're referring to the burns and the blackout, I presume."

Aurick gave me a devastating smile. "Smart, too. You're quite the package."

I put down my fork without taking a bite. "Let's not play these little games. First, I'm not a package, and second, we're both too old for games. You, however, are certainly the oldest one here."

That was a partial lie, seeing as I was the She-Wolf and I didn't know what he was. It was quite possible I was older, but I was enjoying this game immensely. Aurick was fun to spar with. The way his eyes twinkled after every witty retort was addicting, and I enjoyed making that happen.

The package part, however, I was firm on. I'd had my days of waitressing with men grabbing my arms and usually my ass as I walked past their tables. They'd always beg me to stick my finger in their tea to "sweeten" it while I tried not to gag. Oh, wow, I bet that was part of my curse. The *lupa* curse. A wolf and a whore. My fingers clenched around my knife and fork. I hated the gods.

"As you wish. I will try to keep little from you." He took a bite of the lobster and his eyes rolled in the back of his head. "Ava, you must try this before commencing what I expect to be a thorough interrogation of my life."

Aurick picked up a morsel of lobster from his plate and leaned across the table. His hands glowed gold in the flickering candlelight. He smelled smoky and seductive. Dangerously so.

"You want to feed me?" I asked.

"I want you to indulge, Ava Falcetti."

"And you're the one to indulge me?"

Aurick tilted his head. "Would you stop fighting me? What I want is to offer you peeled grapes from my fingertips and pour wine into your mouth dribble by dribble. I want to show you the world and hear about yours. I want to introduce you to the true meaning of pleasure. I promise it would be different with me. Alas, we are not there yet, so I must wait until you are ready."

I swallowed hard. Lord, I was out of practice. "How about we start with the lobster?"

"As you wish."

Without breaking eye contact, I put my mouth around the fork and took the bite. Curses. He was right.

"And?"

"It's incredible. Now, let's start with your first life, shall we?" I said, dabbing my mouth daintily.

He held up his wine glass. "Of course. What would you like to know?" Before I had a chance to consider, he added, "Just remember, this is an equal partnership. So be prepared to answer the same questions."

"Okay. Sort of limiting, don't you think?"

He laughed. "Only if you don't want to share stories about your childhood."

With a grimace, I took a deep swallow of wine. Anything to give me a minute to collect my thoughts. Aurick gave me an interested look. He'd probably already read everything into the gesture, something that would've taken Jim ten sessions with a marriage counselor to figure out.

"You don't like talking about your childhood," Aurick said quietly. "That's fine. Why don't I tell you about mine? I won't ask for yours in return, either. Only that you tell me something about your previous life."

"Okay. I accept that deal."

Aurick smiled. "My family were merchants. Middlemen of the Silk Road. I don't remember much about our life, but I can still smell the myrrh, recall the shape of the colorful triangle flags on our outpost, and feel the softness of the delicate silk of our robes. I saw goods pass that would make exotic dealers green with envy today. Lacquered woods, ivory sculptures, even drugs and dancing girls were traded and sold. Swallow your distaste, if you can."

"I guess the more things change, the more they stay the same."

"Precisely. My family dealt only in silks, however. When I was a boy, it was my job to stand guard over our silks while my parents completed various jobs. I took it very seriously. You can imagine a stern-faced seven-year-old standing with his arms crossed in front of a tent. The hot sun drying out everything for miles, parched with thirst, but ready to die for his job."

I smiled at the picture. "Yes, I can."

"My older brother frequently fell asleep, but I was determined not to get drowsy in the mid-day heat. Men could come up like a mirage, and I was never quite sure if it was a Djinn or a human. The boundaries between natural and supernatural were even weaker than they are today. One particular day, a small man with a pointed beard came up to me. He wanted to know about our wares. I told him to come back when my parents had returned, but he offered me a peach."

"A peach?"

"The golden peaches of Samarkand were so desirable, marriage deals and royal proclamations were cemented with them."

"Those must have been some peaches."

He nodded, watching my eyes as he remembered. "I can still taste the juice as it ran down my fingers and the delicate, fuzzy skin of the fruit."

"That's a wonderful memory," I said, already imagining the last really good peach I ate.

Aurick's eyes darkened and he sat back. I hadn't even realized we'd both moved forward, almost meeting over the center of the table.

"His cronies got away with two baskets of silk while I indulged. I've never had another peach since."

I clapped a hand to my mouth. "Aurick! That's horrible."

He laughed. "It was, but the memory is precious. I can feel the heat of my land and remember what my brother looks like. All of that is worth the memory of shame. I've learned to take the good with the bad."

As I lifted my glass to cheers, I considered the options before me. Being around Luca produced a visceral reaction. Basically, I wanted to jump him, conversation not necessary. Aurick presented a more nuanced experience. The chemistry was there, but it bubbled gently beneath the surface and often got distracted by a stimulating conversation. I could see us arguing about the concept of souls before ending the argument in raunchy sex on the table.

You know, that kind of chemistry.

Chapter Twenty-Six

WE MOVED into the dessert portion of the evening, sitting in a comfortable silence as we finished the bottle of wine and a chocolate tart with crunchy, caramelized hazelnuts on top. Everything had been divine, a feast fit for the gods, who didn't deserve feasts and praise in my mind anyway.

"How long are you staying on Aradia?" I asked. "For your vacation, I mean."

Aurick's eyes sparkled. "I'm not sure. Being supernatural has its perks."

"Unlimited vacation time?"

"Life is but a vacation to supernaturals. Surely you're beginning to find that out for yourself now."

I swirled the last of my wine without drinking. "Why are you so certain I'm something other than a MILF?"

Aurick finished his own glass and sat back to study me. He had folded his napkin over his plate and carefully arranged his knife and fork on top. In the flickering light of our candles, I noticed he was beginning to get fine lines around his eyes, but also that he had this alluring way of raking his hair back with a practiced hand and smiling at the same time. "Because god magic flowed through you."

I thought fast. "Maybe I was a conduit from Thessaly."

"Doubtful. You've handled this rapid flow of information too well."

"Okay," I drew out slowly, knowing we were rapidly approaching the most dangerous part of our little game of chess. "What if I was something supernatural? Is there an international registry for supernatural beings?"

Aurick crossed his knees and laced his fingers over them. He reminded me of the Indiana Jones type. Cultured, yet extremely capable. "Not precisely a registry," he said, "but the Council of Beings does like to keep tabs. We wouldn't want dangerous blood mages or necromancers running unchecked through civilian populations. Whether they be MILF or supernatural."

"We?" I raised my eyebrow.

"The supernatural world in general," he said.

"So you're not on the Council."

"I am not on the Council," Aurick said, enunciating each word carefully.

I tried. I tried really hard to find things wrong with this hunk. But damn if his face wasn't the most sincere, candid face I'd ever met. Frankly, it made me want to spill my guts. *No! He probably can do mind control. Remember how he made Nonna forget about him for a year?*

"Can you control thoughts?" I blurted out.

Aurick coughed. "Mind control, Ava?"

I didn't back down. "Yes. There are stranger things on this island than mind control."

"Is that so?" he murmured, watching me closely. His intense, arctic gray eyes glowed for a straight thirty seconds.

"Aurick? What's going on?"

"How much do you know about the gods and their creations?" he asked.

I shrugged, picking my words carefully. "Elementary-level mythology."

"And yet you took in all of the information about the people in this village and barely batted an eye. Why do you think that is?"

"I'm a gullible sucker looking for a win at all costs?"

Aurick gave me a frown. "This isn't a trick. I don't want to entrap you in anything. I'm merely curious why you think you're so open to the supernatural world."

"Because I had a panic-attack, and I'm actually in the looney bin somewhere and this is a very vivid hallucination."

Aurick sat back, pressing his thumb in the space between his eyes. I found he did that quite often around me. "Are you always this difficult or is it just for me?"

"Honestly? Probably a little of both. You're not exactly an open book yourself, minus that one childhood story."

"Fair enough."

"Does that mean you're going to tell me what you are?" I put my hand over his. It was warm beneath mine, unlike Thessaly's. Did that mean he wasn't a vampire? "I mean what you really are."

Aurick gave me a wry smile. "You're not going to run away screaming, I trust?"

"My new boss is a harpy. They used to kidnap people, you know."

"Very well. I am a mummy."

I made an odd squeaking noise.

"Do you need a moment?"

I held up my hand. "No, no. I'm fine. Continue."

"I told you my family traded on the Silk Road. My

people were Sogdian merchants near the Tarim Basin region. When I died sometime in the fourth century—that's common era—I was laid to rest with gold foil across my forehead and blue beads around my wrists. I had a variety of grave goods buried with me that I still keep, including a few grains of wheat." He pulled three seeds from his pocket and rolled them in the palm of his hand. "Everything was preserved by the salt beds in the desert. I wish I could remember more of my mortal life, but my memories disappeared like a fistful of sand in the wind. All I have are a few of my brother. They are more precious to me than any amount of gold or power."

"Thank you for sharing one with me," I said quietly.

"You're very welcome. I enjoyed doing it. In fact, I haven't shared one in centuries."

His words made my heart rattle around my rib cage like a little bird wanting to escape and give hugs. Maybe kisses. As the She-Wolf, I was older by over a thousand years. What a cradle robbing cougar.

"What about your..." I made a circular motion like I was wrapping, well, a mummy.

"We didn't preserve our bodies as the ancient Egyptians did. I do not require wrappings. Bodies found in the Tarim Basin were merely desiccated by the arid conditions. We are an accident preserved perfectly down to the braids in our hair and the wool on our caps. Even our eyelashes survived the ages. I merely require rest." He grimaced. "A lot of it at my age."

"Wow. I've never heard of that region before."

"As the old saying goes, 'the world will never starve for lack of wonders, but for lack of wonder.'"

That spoke to my soul. I'd been wasting away for years in a suburban home because I'd given up my desire to do anything remotely soul-fulfilling. I had literally starved it of adventure, and I let it happen because it was safer.

All night long, I had felt something kindred stirring in my almost-shriveled soul. Now, in this moment, it strengthened beyond recognition.

Was that check or mate?

Chapter Twenty-Seven

"DID YOU KNOW AURICK IS A MUMMY?"

I was helping Nonna pick walnuts from the yard in order to store them for the winter. The breeze was chilly off the ocean, and I wondered briefly where Thessaly was now that she could walk on land.

Nonna and I had gone through the zucchini and other squash, canning and preserving as we worked through the last of her garden. It was oddly comforting. Despite having never quite taken to domestic life—I relied on Stouffers or the microwave most nights—helping Nonna felt like helping my actual grandmother, whoever she may have been. Like I was finally at her knees, gathering long lost secrets to the universe.

For the last two days, I'd spent my mornings at the bakery learning yeast and my afternoons with Severus's scrolls. Most of the time, nothing happened and many of the pages stayed blank. Despite calling casually for Piero and his lute a few times, he never showed his doublet again, and without his help, I was in the dark. Worse, I wondered if he was stuck in limbo on some weird ghostly plane. Ghosts couldn't possibly die again—right?

Nonna chucked a walnut in her basket. "Ah-ha! I figured something ancient, possibly a bloodsucker, but my eyesight has been getting bad these last few years."

"You said you were certain he wasn't a vampire, that he'd eaten plenty of your garlic bolognese!"

Nonna shrugged. "Nothing is certain. Plus, I couldn't very well tell you that I'd actually stuffed a few cloves up his nose to make sure. You'd just arrived and we barely knew each other."

I didn't ask if she was serious. "He's from the Tarim Basin. Apparently, they're different than linen-wrapped mummies."

Nonna watched me bend down to grab another handful of walnut shells. "A Tarim Basin mummy. Powerful creatures."

"You've heard of them?"

"*Sì*. Maybe you were right. Best forget about mummies and men. Think of your boys."

I knew Nonna was right, but he was someone who made me feel like a lovestruck teenager, which was something I could honestly say I'd never felt before. When I heard his voice, it made me jerk and rub my chest where my heart sped faster. There! I could feel him, even before he spoke.

"Would you like some help picking walnuts?" Aurick asked. He was wearing a linen shirt and tailored slacks with Italian leather shoes. I could see a few curly chest hairs wisping out of the two buttons he left undone at the top. I immediately looked at the sky and squeezed my thighs together.

Nonna handed him a wicker basket. "Be my guest."

"I had a lovely evening the other night," Aurick said

softly so that only I could hear, although with Nonna, you had to operate at jet level proportions to get her to hear anything, especially if she didn't want to respond.

I felt my cheeks go warm again, remembering how we'd walked home from the square, both to the same villa, and how he'd kissed the undersides of my wrists goodnight outside my bedroom door. Hoo boy, let me tell you. That was way more intimate than a kiss on the lips.

"It was interesting," I said judiciously.

Aurick stopped picking walnuts and looped his arm through mine, gently turning me into his chest. It felt like we were the only two in the yard. "Interesting enough to go on a second date?"

I tried to laugh off the intense feeling of intimacy. "You didn't quite figure me out so you need a second try?"

"Or I enjoy your undivided attention."

"You are quite the Casanova," I shot back.

Aurick bent his lips to my ear, his breath and body warm on mine. Goosebumps spread up and down my arms. "Is that a yes?"

I let my body feel all of the adrenaline coursing through me at his proximity and tried to picture the same with Luca. Maybe it was a lack of imagination, but I couldn't. Aurick was igniting different pieces of my mind.

"Yes."

HARPIES DIDN'T MAKE natural teachers, more like natural prison guards. Rosemary only needed a baton or a whip to crack to complete her look. "Not like that!" she barked before smiling at me sheepishly. She was still getting used to the fact that I was probably a terrifying beast who had no idea yet how to control my powers. "Sorry, darling.

Maybe step away from the flour for a second. Let me collect myself."

I held up my hands. "I know it's the harpy talking, but I promise not to do irreparable damage to your shop, even if you turn your head for a second."

"Just the dough," she chided.

I threw a handful of flour at her. It dusted the air as it sailed, way missing its mark. Rosemary wrinkled her nose at the fine powder and sneezed once. Then a second time. Soon, she collapsed in a torrent of sneezing and laughing while I ran to grab the dust pan.

"Okay, darling. You're right. I'll loosen up. After you clean my bakery."

"Fair enough." I began to sweep as Rosemary flicked her wrist, spraying flour out in sheets to roll her pizza dough. This morning's toppings were burrata with eggplant marinated in roasted garlic and olive oil.

"Have you talked to Luca since we ruined your date?" she asked. Her pizza doughs were perfectly fluffy balls of dough.

"Besides that morning in the bakery when he let me use his phone, no."

"Hm. And Aurick?"

I jumped at his name. "Marco told you?"

"Of course. We are incapable of keeping secrets."

"Like, as a supernatural thing or just a madly-in-love thing?"

Rosemary laughed again and covered her dough balls with a damp tea towel. "The love one. Your date sounded romantic. Marco said he made you his lobster special."

"Yes, I loved every bite. You did the hazelnut tart?"

"Guilty."

"Thank you. It was delicious."

"And Aurick?" Rosemary lowered her voice and shot me a sly look. "Was he as delicious as I imagine?"

My cheeks flamed. "We haven't kissed. But the conversation was nice. He's interesting. And a mummy."

"Really?" Rosemary actually stopped her prep work on the bomboloni dough to gape at me.

"Really. He's a Tarim Basin mummy, so he doesn't need wrappings. Just rest."

The front door bell rang. "Hello?" Rosemary called.

No one answered.

"Did you leave the door open?" she asked.

"No, it's locked," I said, just as a cool wind whistled through the kitchen. It ruffled my hair and I shivered, immediately recognizing the familiar feeling. "It's a ghost wind."

"Come close, Ava."

I could hear her breathing grow quicker as I slipped next to her, the familiar questions filling my mind. Was it a friendly ghost or something more sinister? Surely, there had to be deadly ghosts with vengeful intentions in the world.

Rosemary's hand found mine, and she squeezed rather hard. "We'll be fine," she murmured. "But just in case, do you think you can use your mother magic?"

"I don't even know what it is," I whispered back.

"Focus on the flour. See if you can make it grow."

I took a step back, a little surprised. Was that how it worked? Well, her guess was as good as mine. I sucked in a breath and placed my hand on an uncovered ball of pizza dough. On my exhale, it doubled in size. Another inhale. Another exhale. It grew again.

"What's the plan with the dough? Force the ghost into a food coma?"

"You're the She-Wolf!"

"What does that even mean? Wait," I grabbed Rosemary's arm. "I think it's... Piero?"

My Renaissance Romancer hovered into view, but he wasn't all there. Parts of his face had disintegrated, and his legs were almost translucent.

Despite being seriously creeped out, I drew closer. "Piero? Are you okay? Where have you been?"

But Piero simply stared, as if trying to recognize me.

"What about your lute?" I said, trying to jog his memory. He cocked his head to the side, and one of his eyeballs fell out of its socket.

"Oh gross," Rosemary gagged.

His jaw worked back and forth. Finally, he got it to open. "Av...a."

"Yes! It's me, Piero. Are you there?"

"I'm not sure—I." Suddenly, he clawed at his face as more chunks began to disappear, as if his essence was dissolving, winking out of this realm. His screams became clearer as he was sucked away. "No! Don't do it, please, I beg you, Signor!"

And then he was gone.

Chapter Twenty-Eight

BEING part wolf had its advantages, like my new found endurance. Pre-Aradia Ava never could've run back to the villa without stopping. Still, at this pace, everything burned, and my breath came out in heavy clumps, as much from fear as from the exertion.

Rosemary had told me to go find Nonna, but what could she do? Everyone was surprised to see ghosts on Aradia, and no one had a clue what the great evil was or if it would come for the living next.

Right as an idea was taking shape, I skidded into the courtyard and stopped dead in my tracks before the crumbling Venus statue, the one I'd seen on my first day on the island. I sucked in deep breaths of fresh sea air as I stared, almost entranced. She was healing. The stone was knitting itself back together, and now, faint traces of paint peppered her chiton.

The screen door slammed. "Ava?"

I whirled around to see Aurick striding towards me.

"You look like you've seen a ghost."

"Funny you should say that."

Aurick immediately straightened to his full height and took my hands. "What is it? Do you need help?"

In a split second, I decided to trust my gut. Before Jim, I lived by it on the streets and it never failed me. Why I ever abandoned it, I don't know. Now I had to trust that it felt something kindred and kind in this mummy of a man. "Actually Aurick, I have a problem. A big one."

He studied my face with those serious gray eyes, already analyzing the situation. "I'm listening."

"A ghost problem. They're appearing and disappearing, and it's happening more frequently. Have you felt it?"

Aurick's eyebrows turned down for the briefest moment. If I blinked, I would have missed it. "Disappearing? Are you sure?"

"Yes and it looks painful when they do it, too."

"You've seen it happen?"

"It's terrible, like their essence is being ripped apart piece by piece." I twisted my hands together, shaking from adrenaline. "What could do that?"

But Aurick didn't answer. When I looked up, he was glowing, the same arctic gray-blue color I'd seen at dinner. Energy rippled off him in snaps and sparks. "Ava, get inside the villa," he said, his voice low and urgent.

"Excuse me?"

Nonna bolted out of the house, her hair in curlers and her Villa Venus robe fluttering in the breeze. She swung her head around, looking for the disturbance. "Something's coming," she barked.

Aurick nodded and pointed toward the sea. "From there, through the tear in the veil."

I looked in that direction, but try as I could, I couldn't see or feel anything. "You know about the tear?"

Aurick pushed me toward the villa. "Yes. Now Ava,

unless you've miraculously learned how to control your magic, get inside," he ordered. "Nonna, you too."

I inhaled a ragged breath as Aurick flickered between a skeleton and his GQ looks. This was the mummy. He twisted his wrist and tall sheaves of wheat sprang up in a circle around the villa. I stumbled backwards as my own back warmed, finally reacting to whatever was coming. Heat tingled down my shoulders to my arms as the stalks grew thicker and taller than any wheat I'd ever seen.

Aurick jerked his head at me. "Did you mean to do that?"

"I... maybe?" I hedged. I wanted to stay, to help.

"That was your magic, strengthening mine."

I remembered Aurick telling me he kept his grave goods, including seeds of wheat. Now I knew why. For their magic. And my mother magic had nurtured it.

"What's coming?" I whispered.

Nonna had hobbled inside by now and shut the door. She peered through the curtains, searching for the intruders. Something rustled the grain to our left, like it was taunting us.

"What other grave goods do you have in those magic pockets of yours?" I asked.

"My pockets aren't of the magic variety."

"You know what I meant. Just tell me you were buried with a flamethrower."

"It was hundreds of years ago. Fireworks had barely been invented."

"Is that a no to the flamethrower?"

Aurick knelt down and pulled out a statuette from his pocket, a bronze warrior with a tall, conical hat that looked Scythian. He spoke a few words, and the warrior, about a foot high, stretched and yawned. Aurick whispered something else, and it snapped to attention and marched toward the barrier, disappearing into the dense forest of wheat. There was a clang of metal and the bronze soldier came sprinting back, its imitation eyes large with fear.

"Sea serpents," Aurick said grimly.

"Why are they here?"

"Perhaps they found the tear and were hungry. Perhaps someone called them."

The edge of the wheat swayed and rustled as the serpents searched for an opening. "Oh God," I said, pinching my nose. The stench of rotting fish wafted over us, thick and choking. It could peel paint in a pinch.

Aurick gave me a tight smile. "They're primordial beings, here before us, here after us."

"So we don't stop them?"

"No, we merely survive."

I stepped on one of the raised garden beds and got my first look at them. Dark green bodies circled our position, leaving slimy tracks that hissed and steamed. Their heads were worse, with tiny black eyes and beaked noses dripping venom. Long, pale scars shone in the wetness of their bodies from battles long ago. Honestly, it looked like a dragon had mated with an anaconda, and unfortunately, it brought to mind the sculpture I'd been dying to see in Rome—the Laocoön and his sons being strangled by sea serpents. The way my life was going, these two right here were probably responsible for the Iliad myth. Except none of it was actually a myth and now I might actually die.

The very real sea serpents found what they were looking for, a weakness in our wheat barrier, and slithered through a crack in the stalks, their forked tongues searching for anything alive, which apparently was me.

Chapter Twenty-Nine

AURICK STEPPED in front of me, his hands sparking flames. "Ava, I've learned a few tricks over the years. Please get into the villa with Nonna. She can keep you safe."

From the window, Nonna gestured for me to come inside, no doubt cooking up *strega* stuff as we spoke. But I didn't want to. I had faced down ghosts, a killer island, and gazed on the face of a god. I'd received magic and knowledge. I was ready to come into my own. To know who I was. To help.

Okay, so sue me. I also wanted to impress Aurick. I was but mortal.

Right now, he was doing something weird with his hands. He made an intricate gesture, and golden-colored globules dripped from his fingers like molten glass. They twisted and turned in on themselves, forming something oblong that looked suspiciously like a children's balloon. Aurick blew it gently toward the two creatures.

It floated above the wheat stalks, homing in on its target. As it drew near, the serpents reared up, large suckers visible on their stomachs. They looked painful, possibly even deadly, if touched. With a gurgle, they shot venom at the liquid gold, and Aurick's magic thingies instantly dissipated into steam.

"That's not possible," he gasped.

"What do you mean?"

"Those were practically indestructible. I've seen them stop a troll in their tracks."

"Trolls are real?"

Aurick ran a hand through his hair. "I've been weakened. That's the only explanation. It's something on this island. That's why I took so long to recover. Something is calling supernaturals here and destabilizing them."

"It's fine," I murmured, pulling out all of my mom reserves to get us through this. "Maybe I can make the wheat grow thick and entangle them." I waved my arms in front of me. Nothing happened, except for me looking ridiculous. "C'mon," I growled. Where was my fairy godmother or wise old wizard to teach me the ropes?

Suddenly, heat seared up my back, wrapping around my front and down my arms. The wheat grew rapidly, snarling their wet bodies with its sharp edges and trapping them in its hold.

I felt like dancing or howling. I'd really done... Oh, never mind. The serpents thrashed their bodies a few times and broke free without so much as a paper cut.

Aurick stood next to me, both of us tense and ready, come what may.

"Any other grave goods?"

He shook his head. "Technically yes, but my glassware did nothing, and they were among my most powerful."

"That's what those globules were?"

"Yes. Molten glass I can manipulate."

The serpents hissed, slithering closer and destroying everything in their wake. We were next.

I pictured my boys, a lump forming in my throat. "Aurick, I—"

But I was cut off by a spout of water smashing into the serpents. It was as strong as the tides, and they writhed and gurgled in agony as a lithe woman in a chiton landed in front of us, gently stepping off the crest of a wave.

"Thessaly!"

"I can't believe it," Aurick muttered. "The demon came back."

"Of course, she did," I said, as surprised as he was. "I never doubted it for a second."

Thessaly raised the serpents with her water magic and held them over the ground, trapped in her vortex.

She turned to us, her eyes terrifying, her hair raised above her head like Medusa's, who I hoped to never meet in person. It was magnificent. "Aurick, can you fix the tears in the veil?" she asked through gritted shark teeth. "I can't hold them back for long."

"Possibly."

Nonna stood next to us now. "Together we can."

"I can give you at least five minutes." Thessaly gathered herself, arms back, and pushed the serpents like she was launching a shot-put ball. We heard the screeching of the sea beasts, and they were expelled from the shores in a tumble of rancid blubber and hissing spit.

Nonna and Aurick hurried to the edge of the cliff, conversing in low voices. As he passed, Aurick pulled a stalk of wheat and dropped three seeds back into his pocket. The stalk disintegrated, and I glanced around the yard. What wasn't drenched in two inches of water was slimed or covered in scorch marks.

I turned to face the siren. "I thought you were leaving."

"I was, but I sensed something... malicious. Gods, I never want to be wet again!"

"You came back for us?"

Thessaly tried to look indifferent, but I could see past her cold exterior. She had an affinity for me, probably because I listened. I must have been the first person to talk to her in centuries. As I tried to tell Jim a million times, sometimes a woman just needs someone to listen to her and commiserate. Someone she wasn't paying two hundred dollars an hour.

Thessaly smoothed down her hair and avoided eye contact. "It was nothing. I looked at the ocean and I simply did not want to be in it. I wanted to be dry. I will wait here until I feel like swimming again."

"Okay," I said slyly, wrapping my arms around her.

She was stiff as a board. "What are you doing?"

"It's called a hug. I'm showing my gratitude and affection."

Thessaly began to relax under my grip. I didn't have to say anything else as her arms slowly returned the gesture.

Soon, Nonna and Aurick came back from the cliff, weary and dragging. "The veil is patched," Nonna announced.

"It'll hold for now, but it's like putting a Band-Aid on a geyser," Aurick added, thick wrinkles forming at his temples.

I looked between them and read the worry in their eyes. "I should warn the town."

Aurick shook his head. "We can't separate now. It's too dangerous. We don't know if anything else slipped inside. We need to do a proper sweep of the island."

The thought made my stomach twist, but I put on a brave smile. "I'll be okay. I've got the best siren this side of the Mediterranean to protect me."

"At least take this." Aurick reached inside of his non-magical, but pretty darn cool pockets and gave me the world's tiniest waistcoat. It fit perfectly in the palm of my hand, yet despite its size, I could tell it was of the finest quality. Brilliant saffron and gold threads were woven intricately together.

"Another grave good?" I asked.

"Yes. In my mortal life, I clearly loved clothing. I have many, but the waistcoat expands to act like a straitjacket. If you should meet something less potent than a primordial being."

"Like what?"

"Vampires, werewolves, garden gnomes. Whatever."

"Ah, garden gnomes. Right." But I tucked the little jacket into my own pocket.

"What other tricks do you have?"

"Not many. But there is something lurking here. Thessaly is right about the evil inside. I am not a Council member," he stared pointedly at me, willing me to understand his words at dinner were an omission, not an outright lie, "but I was sent here by the Council to investigate strange disturbances around the veil."

I stabbed him in the chest. "You half-truthed me!"

"I should still. There's so much you don't yet understand, but I want you to know the full truth."

"So, are you the Council or not?" I asked him directly.

"Only a hired hand. The Council has known about the tears for a while now. That's why they sent me to investigate, but something attacked me the second I touched Aradia's land. The last thing I did before staggering to my room in the villa was put a protective spell around my body. That way, whenever anyone thought about checking on me, they promptly forgot. It was the best I could do on such short notice."

"I knew it!"

"It wasn't mind control, Ava."

"It amounts to the same thing in my book."

"I'm sorry for misleading you. It hurt to do so." Aurick stood, looking almost as awkward as the first day I saw him. "Ava, before we separate, do you know what you are?"

"I do," I said carefully.

"Tell me then, because it's driving me crazy."

"How do I know I can trust you? You just admitted you work for some shadowy organization."

"Ava…" His voice was low, almost pleading. At my silence, he said, "You've done powerful magic. That sort of thing is going to draw attention. Let me protect you."

"I'm only a wolf," I protested. "The She-Wolf, sure, but I don't have much power."

"The She-Wolf of legend was never known for using magic. Yet you did."

"So?"

"So, everyone will want to know why and how. Not just the Council."

I won't lie. I didn't like the sound of that. "Maybe she hid it at the time."

"She is you."

"I know that, but it's a little confusing at the moment."

Aurick gave me a last, lingering look. "Be smart. Don't engage if you can avoid it. I'd hate to lose you, Ava Falcetti. I'll meet you in town as soon as I can."

Thessaly and I left on Vespas, a warm spot growing in my chest from Aurick's words and a pit gnawing at my stomach from everything else. The situation was accelerating, and I felt helpless to stop it.

Out of the cypress trees to my left, a familiar ghost in crusader armor darted through the trunks to keep up with me, his paunch heaving with effort. It was the Knight.

A stab of panic hit my chest, and I slammed on the

brakes. "What are you doing out of the grove? It's not safe here."

"Signora, I have come to warn you. No one is safe. On the ghostly plane, I hear rumblings of a powerful necromancer. You need to find—" The Knight started to flicker and his face twisted in fright. "He's taking me! He's corralling my essence into a vessel. Help me, Signora! I'm not ready to go!"

"Get back to the ghost plane," I yelled. "Go to the grove and stay there."

"The pull is too strong," he wailed, writhing while his face and armor rusted away.

Something he said made me pause. "What does the vessel look like?" I asked frantically. "Tell me about it!"

"It's bright, like silver and..."

There was a loud popping noise and the Knight disappeared, just like Piero.

Chapter Thirty

THESSALY'S EYES WERE WIDE. "The necromancer is getting stronger. We need to find him, quick."

Something niggled in the back of my mind. One of my earliest conversations with Nonna. "Luca came here ten years ago. That's when Nonna said all of this weirdness began."

"Luca? Who is that?"

"Supposedly the only MILF on the island. But as Coronis said, either he got through in a weak spot or..."

"He's not a MILF," Thessaly finished for me.

I nodded. "I saw a jar at his house. It caught my attention because it was odd. Moss grew on top and a substance bounced around the glass."

"A substance?"

"A silvery one. It looked magical."

She restarted her Vespa. "Sounds like we need to pay this Luca a visit."

Three minutes later, we roared into town, and I pounded on Rosemary's locked door. When nobody answered, I saw the same feeling of foreboding in my heart reflected in Thessaly's eyes. "She's probably on guard at the basilica," I said uneasily.

"Why are you watching the basilica?"

"Thoth sleeps there, under the crypt."

Thessaly recoiled. "On purpose?"

"We have no idea. Only that he's stuck in a sleep cycle."

The siren shivered. "That does not bode well. A god hiding on Aradia? I don't like it. Especially not Thoth."

Thessaly's mouth formed a thin, worried line, but we marched forward, nerves on fire. I took deep, cleansing breaths, hoping it wasn't my last time seeing beautiful Aradia.

I tried ordering myself to stop being fatalistic. I had my siren squad. We were powerful women—a harpy, a demon, a crow-shifter and, apparently, a wolf. But just because we were powerful, didn't mean I wasn't apprehensive. I'd feel better once we found them alive and well.

We turned the corner. Coronis and Rosemary were sitting together by the basilica, their outlines silhouetted against the setting sun. They stood quickly when they saw us, and by their narrowed eyes, I could tell Thessaly's presence surprised them.

Rosemary gave me a fierce hug. "Darling, you smell like…"

"Sea monsters?"

"I was going to say seaweed. What happened?"

"I'll tell you everything once we survive the necromancer."

Rosemary stared, her eyes darting between us. "*Cosa?*"

"Another ghost disappeared," I told her in a rush. "He described an object I saw in Luca's house. I think we need to investigate. Now."

"Luca?" Coronis laughed. "He's harmless."

"I sincerely hope so, but I can't deny the jar. Let's go look. I'll ask to use the phone, and one of you can distract him while the other pokes around."

Rosemary's face whitened as I spoke. "Necromancer? Here? And you want to confront him? *Dio mio*, this is madness. Then what?"

"We'll be subtle and see how he reacts when we find it. Last time…" I cut myself off, remembering our date. He'd jumped in front of the jar so quickly and then drew me into that toe-curling kiss. I'd completely forgotten about everything else. "Last time, he seemed rather protective of it."

"Okay," Rosemary said, flapping her arms. "Okay," she repeated. "Okay."

I took her hands. "It will be fine. It's four against one."

"But a necromancer, darling? They have armies of dead soldiers they can call upon."

I put on a brave face. Since I knew next to nothing about necromancers, it wasn't hard. Ignorance was bliss in this case.

"Thessaly, can you stay here and stand guard? If I'm wrong and Luca is actually a MILF, then he doesn't know he lives on an island full of supernaturals, and well…"

Thessaly crossed her arms. "Is it because I'm blue?"

"Yes. It's hard to be subtle when your friend is the color of the sea. Also your hair is still crackling with energy."

"Your teeth are still pointy, too," Coronis added. "That must have been some battle."

"Fine. I'll stay, but I don't like it. It could be dangerous."

We left her sitting on the steps, a sense of quiet enveloping us. By now, dusk had begun, and a sliver of moon peeked out from over the trees. The last time I'd seen it, I'd freed Thessaly from her curse. An involuntary shiver ran through me as I remembered the feeling of untainted power coursing through my body.

"The moon," I whispered.

"Yes, it's lovely," Coronis said. "But we have bigger problems. Like a possible necromancer."

"No, the moon. It's what supercharged my powers."

"Let's hope you don't have to use them."

We turned a corner and stopped in front of Luca's apartment. From a distance, everything looked normal. No glowing windows, no skeleton army standing guard, no hounds of Hell. In fact, nothing seemed amiss, and I began to wonder if I had been mistaken. Like when Nonna had us break into Rosemary's Bakery.

We stepped onto the porch and the door swung open, creaking eerily on its hinges. "Okay, that was weird," I said.

Rosemary shivered next to me. "Yeah, that gave me the creeps, and I'm a harpy."

A cold wind blew through the door, and I tried to peer inside, but it was black as tar. Then I saw it. A ghost sparked into the room, and I recognized it immediately. The Italian housewife.

She was screaming, tearing at her hair. The agony on her face was unbearable, and I almost looked away. As she fully shimmered into view, I saw for the briefest moment what looked like an oil slick on asphalt on the hottest day of the year. "The veil," I whispered. "Luca is the one causing the veil to tear."

"With his blood magic," Coronis whispered back. "*Dio mio*, how did we not see this?"

"Where is he?" wailed the housewife, and I knew she was talking about the Knight. I hadn't been able to save him.

Without thinking, I ran forward to help. That was my first mistake. The moment I crossed the threshold, I felt a pop, and when I turned around, Coronis and Rosemary were banging on an invisible barrier, unable to enter.

"Come back," they mouthed. "It's too dangerous alone."

But it was too late. A dark, hooded figure stood in a circle of candles, holding the glowing jar as it trapped the essence of the Italian housewife inside. His head snapped up at my arrival, the candles illuminating his face. It was Luca. He barely looked himself. He almost didn't look human at all. His entire bearing had changed. Tall, terrifying, vengeful. His eyes glowed in hatred—or desperation?

"What are you doing here?" he boomed, tucking the jar safely under his arm. "You're early."

"Did you think we had a date tonight?" I asked, utterly confused.

"It doesn't matter. I have all I need. Almost."

Our eyes met, and I recalled the look he gave me at the fountain when our fingers touched. I remembered thinking it read like hunger. It was the same look on his face now. I took a step back at the ferocity of it. It was like watching a starving man staring at a feast before him.

"Luca?" I asked, a waver in my voice. "Please tell me this is some weird kind of yoga."

Luca almost laughed at that. "There's no point in hiding it anymore," he said. "Yes, I'm the necromancer."

I looked back at my friends, still frantically trying to get inside. "And you've been stealing the veil's power to hide your activities."

"It makes a wonderful barrier, especially when it's so concentrated."

"But why? The veil protects the town, and now it's weakening. Those are your friends you're putting at risk."

"All great ideas have a price."

My eyes narrowed. "And what is this great idea you're referencing?"

"You look so much like her."

I gasped, everything finally clicking into place. "You're trying to resurrect your wife?"

"Of course. How could I ever live without her?"

"And the ghosts are what?"

"An excellent source of energy. Now, all I need is a body."

Luca drew a blade across his hand and sprinkled blood over the flame. It hissed as it fell, and cords as thick as my leg shot out of the darkness and wrapped around my chest, pinning my arms to my sides.

"Yours."

Chapter Thirty-One

TURNS OUT, Luca only wanted me for my body after all. I'm not sure if that made Jim right or wrong, but I hated the idea that my last thought was going to be about Jim.

Nope. I would not let that happen.

Luca stalked closer, examining my bonds to make sure I couldn't escape. He tugged here and there, muttering continuously under his breath, but it sounded more like the ravings of a madman than any spell work.

His breath was warm and smelled like salami. I tried not to gag. I couldn't believe I'd ever kissed him. Perhaps I'd die of embarrassment before he got the honor of killing me.

"I don't plan on killing you," he said, as if he could read my thoughts.

"What?"

"I'm not a killer," he said dismissively, as if he were offended I'd even considered the idea. "Plus, it would never work that way. You'll still need to be there to keep the body alive."

"Ummm..." I began, not sure how to respond. "You're expecting me to co-habitate with my own body?"

"She'll be in charge, of course, but you'll be inside. Think of it like a long dream." Luca took his wife's picture out of his pocket, and even from this distance, I could see the similarities. It must have pained him when he turned around at the taverna and spotted me. A tiny part of me felt compassion. If he wasn't a crazy necromancer and all.

"It won't be so bad," he continued. "She's incredible. Eventually, you'll even come to love her yourself."

Was he really mansplaining to me how I was going to feel about all this? I don't think so. "How did she die, Luca? You said it was for you."

He ignored me, but his back stiffened.

"You killed her, didn't you? And now you feel guilty. Was it on purpose?"

"Of course not!" he shouted, the candles reaching higher for a second in response to his anger. "It was an accident."

I grimaced. I'd hoped my hunch wasn't right. A crazy, guilt-ridden man who could call the denizens of death was a dangerous foe indeed.

Luca began to pace. "Our first child was born sickly. We tried everything, but nothing helped. Necromancers don't always raise the dead, you know. Sometimes, we heal or merely commune with the departed. My wife and I decided I would try to heal our daughter before death completely claimed her."

Luca stopped moving to stare at me intently, trying to get me to understand. Like he truly believed I'd jump on board with the whole body-snatching ritual if I grasped the depth of his sadness. "Except, I rarely used my powers. I wasn't prepared when something darker emerged. Something that took them both. I transversed the realms for years before I found my wife's soul. I'm so close now." He dragged a finger down my chin and cupped my face like a lover. "Your sacrifice will never be forgotten, Ava. Perhaps we'll name our next daughter after you."

"That's a really sad story, Luca, but you can't steal someone else's life."

He turned and began putting the finishing touches on his preparations without responding. So the conversation was over.

Without drawing too much attention to myself, I studied my options. Outside, Coronis was pounding at the veil with her powerful beak, but despite the force, it barely made an impact. Clearly, I couldn't count on any help from them until the veil broke.

I had one advantage. Luca didn't know I had powers, and the moon was almost in full view through the tiny window over his sink. A sliver of a moonbeam crept across the planks getting closer to my feet. Soon it would be within reach, and I could use it as a trigger to access my moon magic.

It was a last resort. The only other time I had called on the moon, it almost burned me alive. I got the feeling my body couldn't take another round, but my choices were limited. Would I rather go back to being half-alive? Twenty years with Jim was enough.

The moonbeam crept closer, and I said a silent prayer. To whom, I didn't know, but I asked them to protect my boys and to watch over my new friends on Aradia. I'd miss them, but I also felt the need to protect them.

I took a deep breath. It was time to fight back, to fight against all those men who thought they could take what they wanted from women without their consent. To rise and overcome.

I moved my foot a few inches to the left. The moment

it touched the moonbeam, I felt my whole being supercharge.

Luca felt it too, and his eyes grew wide. "You are not a MILF?"

"No," I said, my body practically crackling with magic. "And you picked the wrong Mamma to mess with."

Something pulsed and the cord binding me began to turn green. As it sprang to life, it unfurled from my body and slithered toward Luca.

He tucked the jar under his arm for protection and shot off a spell. Black smoke poured from his fingers and withered the ends of the vines before they could reach him. The rot traveled along their length getting closer and closer to my body.

"Impressive," he said, smoke continuing to pour from his fingers. "You will make a worthy host."

I ground my teeth together, unable to answer and hold off his magic at the same time. More black tendrils attacked, and I concentrated on keeping them at bay.

But there were too many. As they came, I heard voices whispering and crawling over each other. I got the feeling each tendril represented a ghost forced to do Luca's bidding.

One touched my shoulder. "I'm sorry," I heard it whisper as my skin turned cold.

"Me too," I gritted out.

Others swirled around my body, covering me in a thick ghost fog. The smell of death and rot gagged my senses.

Luca lowered his arms. "You are powerful, Ava. I'll give you that. But I have all the ghosts of Aradia under my control."

He returned to his work as my magic struggled against the ghost bonds. I wracked my brain, trying to remember what I had learned about ghosts since my arrival. I wished

I had my girls here to help me. They could guide me and fight beside me, but they were still stuck outside the veil.

Something dripped on my head. I looked up but didn't see anything. There was another drop. Then a third. The wet rolled down my face and onto my lips. I licked them and they tasted of salt. They tasted of the ocean.

Thessaly.

When I looked up a second time, she was ensconced in the archway of the door with a finger to her lips. She must have bypassed the veil completely by traveling through liminal spaces. Checkmate to the demon.

As subtly as possible, I gestured to my arms. Thessaly nodded and dropped, somersaulting from the ceiling and landing with a slight splash.

I flinched, but Luca was too absorbed in his ritual to replace his wife's soul with mine to notice. I wasn't sure what that would entail, but it didn't sound comfortable. He said I wouldn't die, but would her soul kick mine out eventually? Would there be a battle? I'd like to think my soul wouldn't go down without a fight.

Thessaly finished her examination of my bonds. "The only way to break these," she whispered, "is to break his hold on the ghosts." Then she smiled. "Fortunately, that's something I can do."

She returned to the ceiling, floating above me in a way that only worked for demons. "Don't worry, Ava. You are the She-Wolf of legend, and I am a demon. Together, we are formidable."

I took a deep breath and centered myself. It was time to bring the flood. Literally.

"You know, Luca," I called out. "Death is a kind of liminal space."

"That is true, especially for a necromancer," he

allowed. "The boundary is not as clear as the living believe."

"Then you should've known better."

He stopped his ritual, finally truly surprised. "What should I have known?"

"That demons inhabit boundaries and a veil can always be pierced."

A sharp scream pierced the room. It chilled to the bone.

"What have you summoned?" Luca shouted, whipping his head around.

Thessaly catapulted onto Luca and filled his senses with sea water. Instantly, the ghost hold broke, and I was free.

I lunged for the jar, but even two against one, Luca still had the upper hand because he was willing to do things we wouldn't. His black magic seeped through Thessaly's water, scalding her wherever the droplets hit. She cried out in frustration.

Luca flung Thessaly off of him, and magic sparked from his wrists. She barely managed to dodge his next attack and flew up to the rafters.

"Ouch!" My pocket grew hot, blistering me. Aurick's jacket.

I pulled it out and tossed it in the air while sending a shot of mother magic at Luca's chest. Immediately, the jacket expanded, doubling in size as it clung to him like a little headless torso. It was almost cute.

He screamed as the coat bit into his arms, restraining him as the sleeves tied themselves into a knot behind his back. He was still potent with his mouth, and right now, he was hurling spells that ricocheted around the tiny apartment, blasting books and empty bottles of wine. I needed to creep closer if I wanted to secure the jar from under his arm.

"We are matched, Ava," he yelled. "You felt the sparks. You are meant for me!"

Blood ran down his face, but his eyes were still lit with madness. Like a cornered animal, he seemed more dangerous than ever. He closed his eyes and began to sling spells, chanting at a rate that would make rappers sweat.

"You mean my body. Not me," I corrected him. I powered forward, absorbing spells as I went until I was close enough to grab Luca around the neck. A clear bubble encased him from head to toe. It crackled with energy, giving off scents of sage and juniper. Luca's face screwed up in a rage as he tried to bang his forehead against it to little effect.

"I'm going to need that jar," I grimaced through the pain. Magic leached into my body from the moon. Tiny hairs rose on my arms and neck as Luca howled.

Punching my hand through the bubble felt like sticking my whole arm into a vat of molasses. I grappled for the jar as Luca twisted and turned, held by my magic and Aurick's coat. Inch-by-inch, I pulled it free.

Maybe I should have felt honored that he wanted me for my body. Or maybe just pissed. In fact, I was both of those things, but I was also sad for him. My stupid She-Wolf mother's heart felt his pain deeply. "Luca, I hope you find the tranquility you so desperately need." With that, I smashed the jar to the ground in the middle of his flaming circle.

Silvery wisps escaped like curls of steam in Rosemary's very best latte macchiato. Their voices rang in harmony until they exploded apart, forming the shades of ghosts I knew so well.

Piero had his doublet buttoned in the wrong holes, the

Roman Centurion had lost his sword, and his mastiff howled plaintively at the moon. So many others I had never seen before spilled out of the jar, their essences freed. Finally, the crusading Knight emerged. He looked beleaguered but shot straight toward his woman. They embraced, the Knight crooning and petting her hair as the woman sobbed. If my mind wasn't quickly trying to shut down against the magic coursing through my cells, it would have been sweet.

"I can't hold it much—"

And then, I passed out.

Chapter Thirty-Two

SOMETHING COLD WOKE ME. It seeped into my bones like a damp trickle and invaded my senses. My arms felt like concrete, but the coldness made me want to move, to sit up, and to rub vigorously against the chill.

"She's waking," a strange voice said. "Now stand by while I secure her with the Gordian Knot."

Another voice, blurry but familiar, vibrated in my chest. Aurick. And he was furious. I could hear it in his tone. "It could have waited. I would have vouched for her until she woke naturally from stasis."

"She needs to answer for her crimes," came the response, curt and inhumane.

It felt like he was talking about me, but that wasn't possible. I hadn't committed any crimes.

Vague forms began to take shape in front of me. I saw the stranger bend down, and something biting touched my arms.

I groaned, but the pain disappeared a moment later when Aurick knocked the man's hands away. "Is that necessary?" he snapped. "She can barely open her eyes."

"Be careful, Aurick. You are interfering with official business. She used god magic."

"And as I'm sure you've already noticed, Ava Falcetti is hardly a god."

"Then explain how she did it, because the Council is dying to know."

Out of slitted eyes, I watched the man wave his hand around a slumped figure, bringing it to a floating position. Luca.

That meant I hadn't blacked out for days this time. Whatever that cold substance was, it shocked my whole system into waking only minutes after breaking the jar.

Luca merely looked sad now, like an empty husk. His bloodshot eyes were as hollow as the deep spaces beneath them, bruised and blackened from too little sleep and too much dark magic. Which was kind of how I felt. The Gordian Knot glowed blue on his wrists, and it looked painfully tight.

I turned my head the barest millimeter. Rosemary and Coronis were there, hovering in my peripheral. I didn't see Thessaly. Maybe she was hiding again, waiting.

"Tell the Council we all vouch for her," Rosemary said. "You can't take her away."

"Council matters are not your matters, harpy," the man responded coldly. "Now, if you would all stand back, I would like to finally do my job."

He knelt over me, his long, leather duster brushing my face while he clamped shackles tied in intricate knots to my wrists. They glowed blue on contact. I cried out, my body jerking against their bite, but he didn't loosen them. "Aurick, I suggest you do your duty, too. Take the necromancer to the Council to answer for his crimes."

"This isn't over, Manu," Aurick said. "I will follow Ava to the Council as soon as my duty is done."

"I look forward to sparring with you," Manu replied. "Especially when the Council finds out your mind has been clouded by lust."

Aurick's jaw ticked at that. Wait, did that mean he had feelings for me?

"You're just going to let him take her?" Coronis exclaimed.

"I have no choice. And neither do you," Aurick said. Even from my position, I saw the warning in his eyes.

Then, Nonna came up behind him, and I saw rage in hers. "We'll keep watch over your kids," she promised as Manu jerked me to a floating position next to Luca.

I tried mumbling thank you, but my mouth wasn't working yet. My brain was even further behind, stuck in a fog of extreme fatigue. I had noticed she said kids instead of boys, though. Just in case.

"Wait, I'm not dead," I managed to croak.

"No, Mamma, you're very much alive." Nonna patted me on the hand, and for whatever reason, that little gesture pushed me over the edge and I began to cry. I couldn't help it. I knew it was crazy and that I'd only just met these people, but they had become my family. It didn't matter if one was a demon, or a harpy, or a mummy. They felt like home, something I'd never really had before. I couldn't be arrested now!

"You did good, Mamma. You protected your town."

"We'll find you," Rosemary promised, her face full of anguish. "And get you out of this mess. You still owe me mornings at the bakery!"

That was the last I heard from them before my body bounced, Manu dragging me across a barrier. Away from Aradia, away from reality.

His fingers dug into my bicep as I winced in my fog. "Now, you are mine, godling."

Thank you!

READY TO CONTINUE THE ADVENTURE? Snag the next book in the series, *Making Midlife Madness*, on sale for $3.99 or free in Kindle Unlimited.

IT TOOK Ava forty years to discover her identity. It took the Council ten minutes to decide she was a threat.

I survived my forties long enough to discover I'm cursed. Figuring out how to break the curse is a whole other problem.

My arrival in Aradia set off a series of unexplainable events—the veil breaking down, ghosts arriving by the shipload, and Aurick becoming... beautiful? Now, the dying god has finally started dying, and everyone fears his re-birth.

Fortunately, I have my new found powers and my Siren Squad to help me. Only, I still have no idea how to actually use my powers, and the Council arrested me on sight.

At least, I don't have time to think about my ex or to wallow in my misery. In fact, getting divorced at the age of forty doesn't seem so hard anymore.

There's nothing like an angry archon hell-bent on global destruction to give me a little perspective.

Making Midlife Madness is the second book in Heloise Hull's Forty Is Fabulous adventure series. It's for all those who believe that finding your true powers late in life is a blessing, not a curse—even if it turns out you're actually cursed. If you like Paranormal Women's Fiction or Urban Fantasy, you'll love this series.

. . .

JOIN my newsletter and I'll send you a FREE novella. *Making Midlife Memories: Forty Is Fabulous 1.5* follows Ava as she astral projects with Manu. You're under NO obligation to stay on my newsletter list, but if you do, I promise I'll only send out new release notices and sales/giveaways every few months. Make sure you get the novella by immediately adding me to your contacts and marking "not spam/not junk" from your email carrier. FYI: You can also follow me on Amazon for updates.

NOTE: If you don't read the short story, you won't miss anything in the main arc of *Making Midlife Madness*. It simply deepens the relationship between Ava and the god in the cave. But if you do choose to read it, please know the novella is grittier than Ava's story thus far. Be prepared for blood, sex, glory, and even an ancient Roman recipe for honey fritters. If you're cool with that, then carry on!

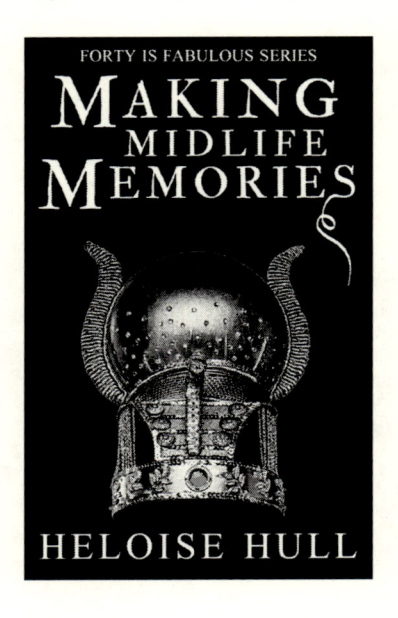

THANK you for taking a chance on a new author! I hope you enjoyed your first ticket to Aradia and are looking forward to your next. If so, please consider leaving a review on Amazon. I know you're inundated with pleas for this all of the time, but it's for a good reason, I promise! Your thoughts and words help other readers find new favorites and help me continue to write. They're extremely important.

Afterword

So how much is true? Believe it or not, most of it! Aradia is the name of a book written in 1899 about a group of Tuscan witches. (And my source material for Nonna's cleansing spray in Chapter 6!) Alternatively, it's the name for the revival of a Tuscan goddess, while Arcadia is, of course, another name for the land of the Fae. Don't worry. It will all play out in books 2, 3, and 4!

As you can tell, I'm fascinated by words and plays on words. The She-Wolf, or *lupa*, means a female wolf in Latin, but it's also slang for a prostitute. The same sort of etymology plays out in the Greek word, *troia*. A female pig, but also a whore. Even English has this overtly misogynistic play on words. *Bitch*. A female dog and, well, you know the other. On one hand, nurturing and on the other, vindictive. Just like a beast. We're taking these words back, friends.

If you're curious about my inspiration for Aurick, search for images of the Yingpan Man. The university website below is an excellent source, but be forewarned of graphic mummy images! Estimated to be nearly 6'6, Yingpan Man was in his mid-fifties when he died at a Silk

Road trading post. The man was extremely wealthy and a "clotheshorse". In fact, he liked fine fabrics so much, that among his many grave goods, he was buried with a miniature chest full of clothing that he kept on his stomach, as well as a bronze, kneeling warrior.

The Scythians, an Eurasian population, played a huge role in the Silk Road with their desirable, delicate metalwork, and the Sogdian merchants' impact on history is only now beginning to come to light. This book, in part, is dedicated to *Scythian Empires* by Andrew Bird. Have a listen and buckle up for an epic second adventure, coming soon!

Penn State University (Yingpan Man.)

Smithsonian Institute (This is a really cool, interactive exhibit of the Sogdians on the Silk Road.)

About the Author

Unlike her namesake of medieval infamy, Heloise doesn't intend to have her midlife crisis in a nunnery. She'd much rather drink espresso martinis and chant in fairy rings while wearing socially questionable clothing.

In her other pen names, Heloise writes romance, nonfiction, and epic fantasy, all with tinges of the ancient world thanks to dual degrees in archaeology and Classics. She splits her time between St. Louis and Chicago with her husband, two kids, and two cats, but is actively plotting how to bring in a puppy.

Made in United States
North Haven, CT
14 June 2025